Shadow's Moon

Season Three

Shadow's Moon Season Three
Ash Rock Series

Contact information: marcellevalentine.com/

Published in the United States of America by Medusa Publishing.

Medusa Publishing is a registered trade name of Medusa Publishing, LLC.

First Edition: 2023

Making the most of it

Shadow's Moon

Ash Rock Series

Marcelle Valentine

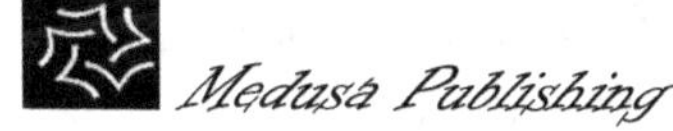

Table of Contents

Episode Fifty-Seven: One Step Back

Shay

I IMAGINE MY decision to leave is confusing to you. Hell, it still baffles me; in truth, it all boils down to one thing…. Moon. She deserves a better life, and I refuse to ever let anyone collar her again.

With Travis's whereabouts unknown, me being all but rejected by my mate, and the fact I exposed my rogue ass to their pack, I figured the most prudent decision was to leave. I wish I had the means to do it without returning to the pack that hates me.

I am acutely aware I am walking into the lion's, or in my case, wolf's den, but Brady keeps promising me everything will be okay. Can anyone say idiot party of one? Yeah, this may not be one of my smartest decisions.

Brady is offering to make me his Luna, but I never wanted to lead, and I still don't want it. I just need to settle some place I can live in peace, release Moon whenever she needs to run, and maybe have a friend or two to share a glass of wine with.

Basically, my only want in life is to be free. Something I experienced for a blip of time in Lake.

Maggie has apologized to me so many times since we left that I'm actually starting to believe her. I never honestly thought she was inherently evil, not like Natashia.... Shit, how in the hell could I forget about Natashia?

"I may have made a mistake," I confess to Brady as I leave the park bench we found on our walk back to the hotel after our late-night dinner. Dropping what remained of my uneaten burger into the trash. My appetite is decreasing the closer we get to Montana.

Or the further we get from Lake, the further we move away from Shadow and Foster. Moon softly interjects.

No, they have nothing to do with this. Listen, my sweet wolf, I know you care for them; I can't.

Why? Why would you not at least talk to them first?

If I have any hope of protecting you, of guarding your heart.... I cannot allow myself to think of what could have been, Moon. I'm sorry that you and Shadow were the two who got hurt in all this. Foster and I were.... We—it was just never going to happen.

But he did come to you. Perhaps we judged him too harshly.

That was just sex. Nothing more. I can feel how heartbroken she is, making me feel like the biggest asshole in the world. I hate knowing I contributed to the pain she now feels. The second I realized who he was, I should have kept moving. If I had done this, Travis never would have found me. I would never have gotten involved with Foster, and my wolf wouldn't be retreating in on herself.

But without them, I wouldn't have a name. Well... Shit, I don't have any comeback to this because she is absolutely right.

"I don't understand. Why?" Brady's question ends my conversation with Moon. Hell, at this point, I'm not entirely sure if she even wants to talk to me anymore. She grows increasingly distant the further we move away from Shadow.

Brady leans over, pulling my attention back to my previous conversation. For the moment, maybe I should let Moon be.

"Brady, it's not just your mom and dad who didn't want me in the pack. Nobody did, especially Travis and Natashia." I tell him as I sit at the opposite end of the bench, twisting my hair in a loose bun.

Sliding over so he can be closer, he drapes his arm on the bench behind me. It's crazy how a few months can change things. I would have been a nervous mess if he had done this prior to me leaving. Now, I just sort of feel defeated.

"Shay, I don't care who likes this or not. They can all go fuck themselves. The only opinion I care about is yours. I hope the only one you care about is mine. I want you, Shay." His admission shocks me, and I think he knows it, resulting in him clearing his throat before elaborating. "To stand beside me and run our pack. I hope you will forgive me in time and find it in your heart to love me because I only want to make your life better than it was before."

"I'm not so sure I can love anyone. Except for Moon."

"Moon?"

"My wolf. You know, the one the pack did not permit me to release, the one who didn't have a name until a few weeks ago because I wasn't told I was supposed to give her one, nor was I given the opportunity to. This is the life they forced us to live. The one, your pack, felt we deserved."

"I can't change what happened in the past, but if you let me, I promise I will change your future. I promise they will not force one more wolf to live like you had to ever again, nor will I allow anyone to hurt you or make you feel you are less than the amazing woman you are. If you give me a chance, I will make you happy."

"Until you find your mate."

"I found my mate. My chosen mate. The woman I would like to spend the rest of my life with. I'm not looking for anyone else." Running his fingers down the side of my cheek, he tilts my chin to ensure he has my undivided attention.

"We can take this as slow or as fast as you want." His eyes drop to my lips, and I instinctively run my tongue over them. Why does it seem almost reflexive to do this when someone focuses their attention on your mouth?

He slowly leans forward, and I can hear Moon whimper, but she needn't worry since Brady is nothing short of the gentleman he promised when he presses a soft kiss to my forehead. Standing, he reaches out, offering his hand to me. Accepting his offer, we stroll slowly back to the hotel, hand in hand. The entire time, I try to shake the feeling that I am taking a gigantic step backward.

I do too, Shay, so can we go home now?

We are going home, Moon.

No, we're not. Lake is our home. Our home is with —

Foster and Shadow?

I was going to say with Seamus, Hyde, Ness, and Finch, but since you brought it up.... Yes, Foster and Shadow too.

Those are just people; they're not our home.

I'm afraid I have to disagree.

Moon, we cannot go back. She does not reply as she has once again grown silent, and I worry the further we move away from them, the more she will end up hating me.

Episode Fifty-Eight: Following

Foster

"NOW IS NOT the time to leave, Foster!" Ian has been trying to convince me to stay for the last hour. He does not understand what we lost when Shay left.

"Sorry, Ian, but I have to do this; the pack will have to survive without me until I get back. While I'm gone, I'll announce to the pack they are to follow you in my stead, and you need to take this time to decide if you still want to step down. You're a damn good Beta. I would be remiss if I didn't try to convince you to stay on."

"Every Beta needs to know when his time has passed. Mine did a long time ago, but I felt obligated to stay on since I couldn't leave the pack in Deacon's grubby hands. I refused to do that. But now, I am free to follow what I know is right. Besides, there may or may not be a certain special lady I would like to spend more time with."

"And Aunt Claire would be fortunate to have you," I tell him, pulling him in for a hug as we clap each other's back.

"I'm glad you think so. Claire is an incredibly special lady, one I have waited an exceedingly long time to ask out, and just when I think my wait is over, you go and shit all over my plans by taking this impromptu trip."

"Ian, you can date my aunt and still run a pack. It's not like I'm leaving forever—"

Unless our mate refuses to return because you are such a dickless wonder. Shadow interrupts.

I really don't need you to start your shit, Furball. I figured you'd be happy we were going after them.

Had you not been such a miserable, blue-balled prick, she never would have left to begin with. I would be happily nestled next to her each and every night. But you had to be the dumbass you always are. In fact, when we find her let me do the talking. You'll probably just screw it all up again with your big dumb mouth.

Yeah, cause smashing them over the head and dragging her back here is such a great fuckin plan.

Hey, one of us needed to come up with a plan. I figured I would improvise....

Well, don't. He growls his displeasure, but I could give a shit less right now. As much as I want Shay to return with us, I will not force her to do anything. She deserves the right to choose, and no one, not even my impatient other half, will take this from her.

"I hope I'll only be gone a few days. A week at the most." I finish telling Ian.

"And Finch can't do this because?" he asks, drawing out the last word.

"Because Finch will be with Foster," he declares as he drops his bag down on the floor in front of Ian, making him shuffle back to avoid it landing on his feet.

"So if both of you are leaving, who in the hell is going to take care of Nessie while you're out gallivanting around?"

"Uhhh, first off, Mr. Man, I am not a monster. Second, I don't need anyone to take care of me, and third, Foss and Finn can do it since I'm going with them." She announces as she bounds into the room.

"No, Ness," I hope my stern response halts any further discussion of her going with us.

"Yes, Foss! Or... I can stay here and tell everyone that you had to leave so fast because you so colossally screwed up with your mate you managed to drive her away in just a couple of months. I'm sure this will evoke real confidence in the pack for their new Alpha."

"Wait, you found your mate?" Ian asks, his shock seeping into the question.

"I—" before I can finish, Ness cuts me off.

"No. Actually, she found him when she practically ran into him at Stooge's."

"Mandy?" Ian questions while his eyes widen at the thought.

"Oh, Goddess, no! If it was Mandy, I would have to smack the shit out of him. It's Shay. Shay is Foster's mate."

"Ness, you can shut up anytime now."

"And you can get your ass in the truck because we need to go; we're losing precious seconds." She reaches down, collecting her bag as she spins and saunters out of the office, yelling over her shoulder, "Shotgun."

"The hell you say," Finch yells back as he snatches his bag and streaks past her. Ian and I listen to them arguing down the steps and out the door. Shaking my head, I slide my wallet into my pocket before reaching for my duffle.

"Shay's really your mate, huh?"

"She is, and because I was too stupid to admit how I felt about her, she left. So you see, my only hope is to find her and beg her to come back," I say to him as Ian follows me outside.

You better beg hard, asshole. Shadow snarls as I climb into the truck.

On our hands and knees if I have to.

*****

"Any idea where you're going, or are you just winging it? Maybe hoping Shadow will sniff her out?" Shadow laughs; apparently, he finds Finn as funny as Finn finds himself.

"No, dipshit, I have a fairly good idea where we are going."

"Fairly good doesn't evoke a lot of confidence in me, Foss," Ness interjects. She is currently leaning over the seat. She's doing it to piss off Finch since he didn't honor the whole "shotgun" thing.

Finn tilts forward so he can grin at me around Ness's head, prompting her to lean further across the seat. It's kind of Finn's fault since he used to do this shit when we were younger once Aunt Claire began letting Ness sit up front.

"So where are we going? Or did you also want to save this as a surprise for us?"

"Montana."

"And you know Shay is going there... how?"

"It's where her old pack is."

"Ah, cuz, I hate to break it to you, but Montana is still a fairly large state. How the hell are we supposed to find one shifter there?" What Finn and Ness don't know is I called Aunt Claire and talked her into telling me where mom went when she left their pack to follow my asshole father. Packs rarely move locations, so as long as her previous pack is not a group of nomads, I know they are within fifty miles of Whitefish. More importantly, I know their pack name and the Alpha's name. And knowing what an arrogant prick my father is, he will never be able to refuse another Alpha showing up in his territory.

Too bad for Tobias; he does not know who I am. Shit, I may be able to deal with two issues while I'm there. Find my mate, win her back, and kill my father. What could be better than this? I would be lying if I didn't admit that the thought of looking him in the eyes when I issue my challenge only to reveal who I really am just before I end him is damn appealing.

Killing the miserable bitch who ordered our death and beat our mate ranks high on my list. Shadow retorts.

I can't say I disagree with him; the thought of making her beg Shay for forgiveness is almost as satisfying as seeing the shock fill his eyes when he realizes the son he tossed away is alive, well, and soon to be the Alpha of two packs.

Drive faster, blue balls. Shadow growls at the prospect of defeating these assholes. Which is why I will let the whole blue balls comment slide this time.

Episode Fifty-Nine: Changes Are Coming

Brady

I CAN'T BELIEVE I actually convinced Shay to come back with me. I truly figured she would just as soon deck me before laughing in my face or, at the very least, tell me to go fuck myself. Knowing Travis tormented her and is the reason she ultimately left has my wolf and me on edge. I wish she would tell me everything that happened between them. But I'm afraid to push too hard; I envision her shutting down if I do, or at the very least, demanding I let her out of the truck.

Maggie is doing everything she can to put her at ease, not to mention make up for all the shit she turned a blind eye to. It's no secret that Maggie has long had a crush on Colton, except for maybe Colt, but he's pretty oblivious when it comes to girls. She was depressed for weeks after they both came of age and realized they were not mates.

I know the only reason Maggie hung around Natashia was that she hoped Tosh would help her win Colt over. If she had only asked me, I would have told her Natashia doesn't do anything that doesn't benefit Natashia.

Natashia does not like to share the limelight with anyone, and as long as Colt never found out about Maggie, then Natashia could keep stringing him along. He told me more than once how friendly she acted towards him when they were alone, even though she repeatedly told him how jealous I would be if I found out. Let me assure you, nothing could be further from the truth.

If anything, I would have told my buddy he deserves better than her, especially since I know she is sleeping with Travis too.

"Shay, I hope you're not mad that I told Brady what bus you got on." I can barely hear their conversation out here. I stepped out to check my messages, leaving Shay and Maggie alone for the first time.

"Did you tell him the same day I left?"

"No. I swear it wasn't until after Brady had figured it out that I told him, and only after I was confident he would do everything he could to make things right with you."

"Does he know what Travis did?" I know I shouldn't be listening to this, but if what I am starting to believe he did is true, I need to know so I can justifiably kill the bastard.

"I didn't tell him why you left, but I think he is starting to suspect."

Shay sighs, "Damn it."

"I'm sorry you had to go through all this shit. We should have protected you; should have stopped Travis from—"

Needing to know the truth, I storm through the door. "Stopped Travis from doing what?"

Horror crosses Shay's face, realizing I heard at least part of their conversation. When Shay closes her eyes, I have my answer. Dropping to my knees before her, I pull her into my arms and softly say, "You don't have to answer that, Shay. I'm sorry I failed you."

I stay with Shay until she falls asleep; slipping out of the room, I call Colton to find out if Travis has returned or if he's heard from him. I fully intend to have our sentinels detain him until I get back. He will answer for what he did to Shay, but I also need to investigate him as the thief.

"Brady, is everything okay?"

"Yeah, I'm on my way back. Did Travis ever show back up?"

"Nah, but you know him; he probably met some girl and is holding up with her in some sleazy motel. After he's had enough of her, he'll come sauntering back with all the details to rub in our faces, or more likely, just my face." You got one part right, Colt, but what you should have said is when he is all done using her up.

"He hasn't called you, texted, nothing?"

"No. If he was going to call anyone, it would definitely be you. Are you sure everything's okay?"

"Listen, if he shows up, will you do me a favor and let me know he's back?"

"Did Travis do something?" I think Colt is trustworthy, but I don't want to give Travis any sign that I suspect anything. I know if I tell our sentinels to detain him, they will without question. I can't say the same for Coltan.

"No, it's just not like him not to contact me. I want to make sure nothing crazy happened to him." At least not until I'm the one doing it.

"Alright, man, will do."

Thanks, Colt. See you in a day or two." I have no intention of dragging Shay back to our territory until my dad has relinquished his reign to me. Then and only then will I reveal to all of them who their new Luna is, and they better get on board with it, or they can learn what it's like to be rogue.

We should have claimed her a long time ago.

I know, Shade. My wolf is right, but I wasn't brave enough to do it. My dumb ass was too worried about what everyone would say. Thinking back to my conversation with Ophelia and

Nan, it seems many people in the pack felt the same where Shay is concerned. Damn it. All of this could have been avoided if any of us had grown a damn backbone. Me included.

He's hit her.

I know.

He's hurt her

I know.

He raped —

God damn it, Shade, I fuckin know. Fury gets the better of me. Without thinking about where I am and without moving to a more secluded area, I yank my shirt and pants off to release my wolf. I may not have done shit to help her before, but moving forward, I will protect Shay with my life.

And mine too. Shade confirms.

Episode Sixty: Regrets

Shay

I HATE THAT they both know what happened because I find nothing but pity looking back at me. For shit's sake, not only did he take my dignity, but he made me someone to pity. Not to mention Moon has gone completely quiet.

Did I make the right choice when I left, or is my wolf right? Should I have stayed and demanded answers? If I had, maybe Moon could accept my decision, so we could have moved on. Moved past them together; now, I fear I may have lost Moon too.

Traveling back does not give me the same sense I had when we left. And every second that ticks by on the clock is another second I regret my decision. It's like a countdown, one flashing second at a time. When the Moon Goddess tallies up the quality of my life, will I look back merely to realize I only get a few lousy months?

Fuck, I'm a damn idiot.

"Brady," I mumble.

He looks over at me with a grin, but when he sees my face twisted with misery, brows pulled together, and corners of my mouth turning down in a frown as I pick at a string on my jeans, he immediately reaches out for me.

"What's the matter, Shay."

"I think—I think I made a mistake. A horrible mistake. I'm so sorry, but I no longer belong here."

"There are more people in the pack than you realize who recognize how poorly we treated you. You returning with me is the first step to fixing all the shit that's wrong with this pack, and when I choose you as my Luna—"

"That's just it; I never wanted to be a leader, let alone Luna. I don't know any of the things a good Luna should do."

"Are you kidding me? Shay, you would be the best kind of Luna. You're thoughtful, compassionate, loyal, and protective. You know how our wolves and their human counterparts should be treated. Honestly, I am in awe of you."

"Seriously, Brady—"

"I am being serious. Oh, and did I mention I find you breathtakingly beautiful?"

"I call bullshit on that," I tell him with a laugh as I push him back from me. I would be lying if I didn't admit the smile he grants me makes my heart rate quicken.

"Will you do me a favor?"

"I'm not sure what I can do for you, but if I can.... I will."

"Just think about it. That's all I ask. I don't plan on taking you back to the pack right away. I know you're not ready for that, and I need to clean some shit up before I would risk you being there. I planned on putting you in a hotel far enough away from the pack so no one notices you but close enough for me to get to you in an emergency. You'll need to keep a low profile during the day, but I made sure there are woods behind the motel so you can release Moon at night. If you don't want to rejoin the pack after I clean everything up, I will take you anywhere you want to go and set you up with a place to stay until you can get back on your feet. Are you willing to give me a few weeks?"

"Why would you do all this?"

"Because I hope to be an Alpha my pack can count on, and even if you don't think of yourself as a member of the pack, you are an important one to me. So I will do everything and anything in my power to guarantee your happiness."

Biting on my lower lip while I think about what he is offering, Brady pulls the truck to the side of the road before he turns to face me, "Or I can take you anywhere you want to go right now. Shay, I meant what I said. I want you to be happy."

"I'll stay." He brings my hand up to his mouth before kissing it softly. For the rest of the ride to the hotel, he kept my hand held securely in his. The act is a silent reassurance that if I change my mind at any time, for any reason, he will honor his promise and take me where ever I want to go. I know Moon is praying I would choose Lake, but like the pack I ran from, I'm not so sure I belong there any more than I belong here.

*****

I remain in the truck with my hood pulled up, concealing my features, while Maggie and Brady book me into my room. I'm ready to be out of this truck, but more than that, I need to be by myself. I have a lot to consider, and I don't feel like I can do that with them, with Brady, worrying every second about what choice I'm going to make.

If I plan on being true to what I want, I need to make this decision for Moon and myself, and only Moon and myself. I can't worry about what will happen to the pack that never wanted me, the mate who could give a shit less about me, or the fucker who wants to possess me. I need to make a decision we can both live with.

Brady carries the bag I packed into the room while Maggie and I take in the few bags of food we stopped at the store to pick up. Maggie jots her and Brady's cell numbers down on the paper by the phone before she tentatively hugs me and slips out to wait for Brady at his truck.

"Are you sure you'll be okay here? I can always get another room for Maggie."

"No, she'd probably be recognized before I would. I'll be fine." Brady hesitates, his hand on the doorknob, head dropped.

"I will never be able to tell you enough how sorry I am. It's a testament to your character that you agreed to speak to me again, let alone forgive me."

"Do you want to make it up to me?"

Crossing the room, he lifts my chin to look directly at me before softly confessing, "Anything. I would do anything to make this up to you."

"Make sure this never happens to another shifter in your pack. Please make sure you are an Alpha they can turn to when they need you. If you do that, Brady, then...."

"I will live every day making sure I am that man." Slowly he leans down, bringing his mouth inches from mine. "You truly are an amazing woman." When he bridges the last remnant of space between us, his kiss at first is sweet and tender, yet the longer we remain in this moment, it builds to a much more passionate need.

The kiss brings back memories of when Foster kissed me, but it is not all-consuming like his kiss was. Where Foster's was demanding, Brady's is giving. Where Foster's was filled with desire, Brady's is a promise of passion.

My problem is that as much as I want to wipe Foster from my memory, this kiss makes me want him more. I want him to dominate me, tell me what to do, and demand I tell him what I want him to do to me.

This kiss makes me realize one thing... I don't want passionate. I want all-consuming.

I want Foster.

Too bad Foster doesn't want me.

Episode Sixty-One: Determined

Foster

PULLING INTO WHITEFISH, I know I'm within fifty miles of my father's pack; the issue is I am not sure where to go from here. Based on Whitefish's topography, if I had to guess, the pack would most likely be to the north, but that is still a large patch of land to check.

If possible, I would prefer to go in as a man, not as a wolf. Going onto their land as Shadow would be considered an act of aggression, a direct threat to their pack. If an Alpha is worth a shit, this will not go unanswered, meaning they would have their sentinels on us before we got close to the main living area.

I know this is the reason Shay was so afraid when she was on our pack land. What she didn't realize was Deacon didn't give a shit about protecting the pack, so he assigned most of the sentinels to be his personal protection when he traveled rather than what we intended them to be used for.

"Okay, Whitefish," Finn says loud enough to wake a sleeping Ness in the back seat. Halfway through our journey to Montana, she realized the value of sitting in the back instead of in the front since she had the entire area to stretch out in. Finn even tried to swap out, but she flat-out rebuffed this, even going so far as refusing to get out of the truck when we stopped for gas or snacks.

"About damn time," she dramatically yawns as she stretches her arms and legs. "How did you sleep up there in that tiny space, Finny-Finn?"

"Like a baby, little sis, but just so you know, I call back seat for the journey home."

"Duh, we'll both be back here, dumb-dumb. That way Foster can sit by his mate."

"Are you two done yet? Because if you are, we need—"

"Oh, hold on a minute, man," Finn cuts in as he puts down the window.

"Finch, I'm freezing back here. What are you doing?"

"Putting the window down so Shadow can take a big whiff. A big desperately seeking Shay whiff. Go ahead, big guy, sniff away."

I groan when Shadow joins in with Finn's obnoxious laughter.

Yeah, blue balls, let me have a whiff.

If you don't mind your step, you won't be sniffing shit for a very long time, furball.

Not true because I fully intend on inhaling the wonderful scent of Shay the second I see her.

Not if you keep this shit up. Oh, and if you keep calling me blue balls, you'll have no balls because I'm going to have your ass neutered.

Go ahead, dumbass, because what you do to me happens to you too. I can live with changing your name to no balls. Are you ready to never have Shay again? I'm betting not. A low growl rumbles through me, knowing he's right, and he called my bluff.

Yeah, I didn't think so. Better luck next time, blue balls.

Ness whacks Finn on the back of the head as she reaches past him to put the window back up prior to turning her attention to me. "Alright, so where are we going first, Foss?"

"I thought we could grab something to eat before finding a hotel in the area. Then I'm not sure."

"Winging it. Hell yeah, I'm totally down with this plan." Finn is just beginning to reign in his laughter from his last comment, but this starts his hysterics all over again.

*****

Three days later, we are no closer to finding Shay, the pack, or my useless fucking father. I admit I could have thought this through better before just driving several states away, hoping for the best.

The first night we arrived at Whitefish, we found a little diner; the waitress was only too happy to tell us about the hotel just down the road from the restaurant. In fact, she made it sound like it was the only place to stay within a hundred miles of Whitefish, but I think that may have more to do with her flirting with Finch and me.

I do not know why any girl would think it's a good idea to do this. Finn and I have always had one hard and fast rule about girls. If a girl shows interest in both of us, then neither of us will date her. It kept my cousin and me from fighting over the opposite sex during our hormone-driven teen years.

After she walked away, an older guy at the next booth spun around to tell us there was also a motel about thirty minutes outside Whitefish, and it was about fifty dollars cheaper per night. I opted to stay at the motel down the road, hoping the proximity would provide us a better chance of finding what we came all this way for. This has not been the case.

Ness and I have both called the cell phone I gave her several times, but it always goes straight to voicemail. Tired of waiting around for the pack or, better yet, Shay to somehow fall into my lap magically, I snuck out after Foss and Ness fell asleep to search the woods surrounding us.

I made it up to a lake, where I stood on a rocky outcrop for close to an hour. Thinking about the first time I saw Moon and how beautiful she was lying next to the stream. How the moonlight danced across her stark white fur, about the peaceful moment I secretly shared with her until something spooked her and sent her scrambling into the thicket.

Yeah, this thought keeps playing on repeat, but that is not what I came out here for. I wanted to find signs of their pack but never came across anything to point me in their direction, let alone sensed any other wolves nearby.

I took a chance yesterday when we went into the diner to ask Ginny, the flirty waitress who still hasn't figured out that neither of us has any plans on taking her up on her not-so-subtle advances, if she knew Tobias. Unfortunately, she did not know who he was or where we could find him. If something doesn't happen soon, I will have no choice but to shift and hope I stumble onto their land.

My break comes by way of a bleach blonde who talks too much.

"I'm getting tired of his moody ass. He hasn't so much as looked at me since he came back from his secret trip."

"Where do you think he went to?"

"No fuckin' idea. The only thing I know is that when he came back, he was acting all broody and shit. I even cornered him the other day in his office and offered to give him head."

"Ooooh, give me all the details."

"Details? Haven't you been listening to me, Sadie? He turned me down. Me. The best fuck he could ever hope to have. And the asshole turned me down flat. Hell, he even went so far as to roll his damn eyes before he left me on my knees alone in his damn office." I tried to ignore their conversation, not giving two shits about her sex life until I heard her next remark. She may have dropped her tone, hoping no one was listening to her, but my wolf tunes in instantly....

"I could give a shit less if he is supposed to be the next Alpha. No one turns down Natashia Adams. No one. I turn down Alphas; they do not turn me down."

"Bingo."

Episode Sixty-Two: Keeping my Promise

Shay

MY FIRST NIGHT here was probably the easiest night by far. Moon allowed me to release her after Brady left until I realized she was running south. Directly back towards Lake and straight back to them. When I forced her to return to the hotel, she shut down and has not talked to me since.

I miss her terribly, but we promised Brady we would give him a few weeks, and I fully intend to keep my promise.

I have watched all the daytime television I can manage without my IQ dropping. Brady left me some money the other night when he brought more groceries. The mini fridge in my room will only hold so much. He initially planned on visiting every couple of days to get me supplies, yet if I ventured a guess, he also wanted to ensure I was safe and still here.

I told him I would give him a few weeks, but let's face it, people often say things they don't mean and make promises they have no intention of fulfilling. The relief washing over him each time I open the door to let him in is apparent.

This is why I was so surprised when he told me he would leave money for me to get groceries for the next week because he would not be back until Saturday at the earliest.

I guess Adela is becoming suspicious he is sneaking away to see someone. She even went so far as to accuse Maggie of being the secret rendezvous, which would never do in Adela's eyes. In her opinion, he could screw her all he wanted as long as no one found out. But Maggie would never be good enough for her soon-to-be Alpha son. After all, Maggie was nothing more than a Delta's daughter.

In fact, Colton told Brady Adela was so insistent regarding their tryst that the last time Brady slipped away to come to see me, she demanded Tobias help her search Maggie's room. I would have loved to have been a fly on the wall when she stormed into Maggie's room bitching about her, only to discover Maggie sitting on her bed reading a book. Adela attempted to cover her ass by screaming it was merely a coincidence until Maggie could prove she was on pack land or at work the previous two times Brady disappeared.

I guess Tobias was furious and told Adela he was sick of her fucking games. His roared response was that he didn't have time to entertain her ridiculous assumptions could be heard throughout the place. He also didn't stick around long enough to listen to what she had to say because he stormed out of Maggie's room, leaving Adela to face the woman she made the accusation about alone. Had it been anyone else, they would have been mortified, not Adela. She turned it around on Maggie, telling her to stay away from her son and get her ass back to work. Tobias made his opinion on the subject loud and clear when he did not return home, opting to stay at the pack house.

So, back to the money. Brady wanted to make sure I had cash on hand to buy whatever I needed until he could come back to see me. I tried to tell him I didn't need it, but he wouldn't listen.

After a quick shower, I pull my mass of messy hair up, tucking it inside my hood before heading into the heart of this town. I need to get a few supplies, and I plan on getting a book to read while I'm here. I wish I had a library card I could use to get a book instead of wasting what little money I have left in my account buying one since I have no intention of using Brady's money.

I know I am a fair distance from the pack; nevertheless, it does nothing to calm the uneasy feeling I have being out here in the open. I knew coming back was a risk, yet I came anyway.

The only good thing about possibly exposing myself is I feel Moon stirring.

Hi. I tentatively say, afraid that even though she is concerned with my safety, it is still not enough to make her want to talk with me.

Hi Shay. Hearing her voice ringing through my thoughts is the sweetest sound I have heard in a long time.

Are you... feeling better?

I was not sick. Not once has she ever been this clipped with her responses to me.

Fair enough. I've missed you, Moon. She sighs. I know she doesn't enjoy cutting me out any more than I want to deny her. She is simply dealing with this shit situation the only way she knows how.

I have been with you the entire time. I never leave you.

But you shut me out. My world has been entirely too quiet without you to share everything with.

I imagine watching those ridiculous talk shows all day is no substitute. I can still hear people chanting that man's name in my head.

Did you just make a joke, Moon?

I guess I did. I can feel her preen when she hears me laugh. The people around are all looking at me like I'm insane, but I don't care because Moon is back, and she's talking to me again.

I have no desire to return to the stuffy motel room anytime soon, so instead of going to get groceries, I elect to visit the library. I may not have the card necessary to check out books, but I can read them here. The first book I grabbed is a thriller about a maid being framed for her boss's murder. I know I technically wasn't a maid, but I certainly felt like one.

Twenty minutes into this pulse-pounding book, movement on the other side of the window draws my attention. Glancing from the corner of my eye, I discover a shifter I have seen around the pack on a few occasions, standing on the other side of the window. What is most disturbing is he is looking directly at me. I may have only seen him a handful of times, but I am sure he is from Sebastian's pack. I don't know his name, but if I recognize him, I'm sure he recognizes me. My only saving grace is I don't think he can place where he knows me from.

When he moves towards the entrance, I tug my hood closer around my face as I get up to return the book I was reading. It is time for me to get my ass back to the motel.

"Hey." When I do not stop or acknowledge him, he yells again. Hasn't anyone ever told him he needs to use his quiet voice in a library?

"Hey, you. Girl, don't I know you?" The librarian shushes him, but he doesn't seem to care.

"No—no. I don't know you," I muttered, returning the book to the shelf.

"Bullshit. I know I know you from somewhere."

"Sir, you will need to lower your voice, or you will have to leave the library." He ignores her, following me down the aisle. Shit, I am in trouble if he figures out where he knows me from. I'm sure my name is well known throughout his pack since Sebastian and Tobias are brothers.

The next sound I hear has my heart jumping into my throat because it is the last thing I expect around here.

"Evan, what the hell are you doing in here?"

"Gentlemen, this is a library, not a bar. If you wish to remain here, I suggest you lower your voice."

"Or what? What the hell are you going to do about it, you fucking old windbag?"

It's Travis, and no one will ever find me again if he discovers me here.

Episode Sixty-Three: A Way In

Foster

I CAN'T STOP the grin I give Ness and Finch. Thankfully, Ness realizes I stand a better chance of getting what I want from them if she's not sitting with us; as a result, she gathers her stuff as she prepares to leave.

"How do you want to play this, Foss? Approach them or wait for them to approach us."

"Oh, allow me, gentlemen," Ness says as she slides out of the booth and ambles over to where they are sitting. I watch as she says something to the chick who thinks entirely too highly of herself. Both women at the booth look around Nessie before a beaming smile replaces the scowl the bitchy one had covering her face when my cousin first walked up to them. Ness looks over her shoulder at us, mouthing, *you're welcome* before she turns and walks out of the diner.

Ms. High and Mighty stands, adjusting her breast, which I never really understood why girls do this, before strutting in our direction. I do not know what Ness said to them, but if the look in her eyes is anything to go by, I would have to say the word attracted was a part of their conversation.

"Hello, gentlemen," she purrs. "Care if we join you?"

I give her a lopsided grin as I slide over, making room for the girl who will lead me straight to my mate.

The one doing all the talking slides into the booth next to me while the other girl takes the open seat next to Finn. I glance up, finding Ness in my truck, kicked back with her feet up on the dash; yeah, I'm gonna have to tell her about that shit. She is reading one of those girly magazines she picked up during our trip here. When she looks up and sees me watching her, she blows me a kiss, looking entirely too pleased with herself to see her little plan worked.

"My name's Natashia, and this is Sadie." Sadie smiles and opens her mouth to say something, but Natashia cuts her off. "What are your names?"

"I'm Foster." I feel no need to introduce my cousin; he has a working mouth and can answer this for himself, and unlike Natashia, I don't live to hear the sound of my own voice.

"My name is Finch." I know Finn doesn't care for these girls because normally, he would have followed up after telling them his given name with, *but everyone calls me Finn*. Natashia follows my line-of-sight straight out to Ness.

"Who's she?"

"Family."

"Oh, yeah?" she asks as she moves closer to me.

"Mmm-hmm," I advise, shifting my eyes toward her. If this chick represents the assholes Shay had to deal with her whole life, no wonder she left.

"How are you related?"

Finn and I answer simultaneously, "My sister." "Cousin."

"Well, my–my–my, how wonderfully delightful," she purrs, running her perfectly manicured nail up my arm. The unwelcome contact has me dropping my eyes to follow her progress, and I have to work hard to suppress a shudder of revulsion. Shadow mimics my reaction with a growl of his own.

If I remember correctly, this bitch is one of the people who made our Shay's life a living hell.

Means to an end, Shadow. She is nothing more than a means to an end.

Still, I would rather knock her ass off the seat. And what the fuck is that smell? Now, this is something I can do for him.

"You smell—"

"Delicious?" she interjects. If this chick moves any closer to me, she will be on my lap soon. Besides, delicious is definitely not what I would go with.... I was going to go with interesting.

I would have gone with shit. Shadow's snide response almost makes me laugh.

Or shit, I suppose shit probably explains it better than interesting. Instead of letting Shadow respond, I keep my mouth shut, knowing this chick will tell me without me uttering another word.

"It's okay, handsome. You don't have to say anything." She leans so close her lips brush against the shell of my ear. "It's called Desire."

"You don't say."

They missed the mark there because it should be named Repulsion. Maybe we should send this recommendation to the dumbass who sells this shit. This time I cannot suppress the grin his comment evokes. Thank Goddess, this chick believes it was in response to her.

For the next fifteen minutes, she talks nonstop. The rest of us can barely get a word in edge-wise. Ness keeps looking up with a shit-eating grin, making me wonder what she said to these two to prompt them to come up to us.

I don't understand why Shay ever felt inferior to this girl; she doesn't hold a candle to my mate. This girl has to pile pounds of make-up on her face, buy the most expensive clothes, have her hair perfectly styled, and have her nails freshly manicured to look half as good as my beautiful mate. Because the simple truth is Shay looks great in an old t-shirt and holey jeans, with her hair pulled back or laying loose around her face without a stitch of make-up on. Even if Shay wasn't my mate, I would still be drawn to her over this fake girl sitting next to me. I find Shay's easy-going nature extremely sexy. This girl is anything but.

"Are you just passing through?" Here's my opening. Even though she plays herself off as the stereotypical dumb blonde, I know she is much more intelligent than she leads on.

"No, we're here for business."

"Business? In Whitefish? Nobody comes to Whitefish for business." She may laugh, but I do not miss the subtle shift of suspicion filling her eyes.

"Not in Whitefish."

"So if not in Whitefish, then where?"

"Nearby." My vague response would be how one of my kind would answer questions if they were unsure or wary of the individuals we are talking to.

"Not much of anything near here."

"I'm not here for a place; I'm here to meet with a person."

"Hey, maybe you might know him," Finch calmly interjects. "The guy we're here to meet with is a fellow named Tobias."

"Tobias?"

"Yeah, he has a small…." Finn clears his throat and drops his voice to keep up the act before finishing. "Community called Half Crest."

Natashia continues to regard us with marked distrust. The one I figured would tell us everything I need to know speaks up immediately.

"No kidding, we're from Half Crest." Sadie, I knew your helpful people-pleasing nature would assist me in furthering this little plan of mine. Natashia whips her head in Sadie's direction, and I swear to the goddess if looks could kill, this poor girl would be dead.

Hoping to ease Natashia's apprehension, Finn leans forward and murmurs, "Wait, if you're from Half Crest, then you're both...." Finn makes a show of looking around, pretending to ensure no one is close enough to be eavesdropping on our conversation. Once he has the girls thoroughly convinced that he is confident we are not being listened to, he leans closer, beckoning them to follow suit before mouthing, "Shifters."

"You two are...." Sadie mimics Finn by dropping her voice before repeating, "shifters too?"

"Not only are we shifters, but my cuz here is the Alpha of our pack."

Hearing I'm an Alpha has Natashia changing her tune with us. Pressing up against me, she asks me if it is true, to which I grin and reply, "What do you think?"

"I knew there was something special about you. So where is your pack located?"

"Colorado."

"No kidding. If I'm not mistaken, several of our pack members recently traveled there, so this can't be a coincidence. Maybe they went there to meet with you?"

"Sorry, but you two are the first ones from your," I stop myself from saying pack when our waitress suddenly appeared at our booth to check up on us. "Community I've met."

They both gush, and now that Natashia knows I'm an Alpha, she hasn't taken her hands off me. I don't know if she believes this will win me over. I can assure you there aren't many Alphas I know who would want their Luna acting like this. At least not in public.

It only takes five more minutes before she tells us how fortunate we were to meet the best she-wolf in the pack first; after all, who could better represent the best of her pack if not her? I can only half argue with her sentiment since Shay, not Natashia, was the first she-wolf I met, and I was fortunate that time. The Natashia representing her pack thing, I would beg to differ.

Finally, after she finishes patting herself on the back, she offers me exactly what I was hoping for.

It doesn't surprise me when Natashia gets up, leaving her bill unpaid as she sashays out to her car.

"Does that bitch really expect you to pay for their food?"

"Small price to pay, Finn." Especially since she just invited the wolf to follow her into the sheep's pasture.

Episode Sixty-Four: Cornered

Shay

"WHAT THE FUCK are you doing in here?"

"I saw this chick—"

"Wait, you mean you have me standing out there waiting on your dumb ass while you're in here fucking flirting with some dumb bitch?"

"I wasn't flirting. I thought I recognized her."

"From where?"

"Your pack."

"My pack, as in Half Crest?"

"Do you have another pack I don't know about?" His smart-ass response will not go unpunished by Travis, and I think this becomes clear to the asshole who found me when a low growl fills the quiet space.

I am currently hiding at the end of a bookshelf. I know I can't just stand here all day because it will only be a matter of seconds before Travis's irritation subsides, only to be replaced with curiosity about who the pack member could have been. Especially since whoever it was seemed to have disappeared.

When they move further into the aisle, bringing them closer to me, I sprint towards a side door and slip through just before they come into view. Closing it slowly so it does not slam shut and risk drawing their attention to my location, I jog towards the back of the library and cut behind a house just as the door flies open.

“Well, where the fuck is she?”

“Dunno.”

“You don’t know where she went. You don’t know what she looked like. You didn’t know who she was. Tell me this, Evan. What fucking good are you?” I don’t wait around to hear his response.

Taking the most direct route possible to get me back to the motel, I know this little venture in trust is done. Tonight I am getting the hell out of here before I end up collared again. I only make it halfway back to the motel when Moon’s warning sends me scurrying.

Get off the road right now, Shay. Her tone is verging on the edge of panic.

Not willing to ignore her warnings, I dive under a porch just as a car comes around the corner. There is nothing particularly interesting about it. I don’t think I’ve ever seen it before today, but the closer it gets, I know that Moon just saved my life once again because who I find looking out the passenger window is none other than Travis.

The speed they are traveling leaves little doubt they are searching for me. I can’t say if they are looking for some random girl he saw in the library or if Travis figured out the girl he discovered in the library was actually me, and now they are hunting for yours truly. It doesn’t matter either way because I have no intention of finding out.

When I finally crawl out from under that porch, instead of running blindly down the main streets, I cut through yard after yard until I am behind the motel. Sneaking around the last corner before I can return to the safety of my room, I run straight into Maggie.

"Maggie? What—what are you doing here?"

"Shay, do you trust me?"

"Can we continue this conversation in my room?" I ask, looking over my shoulder, expecting the car that holds my tormentor to come into view any second now.

"Shay. Do. You. Trust. Me?"

"Yes," I reply hesitantly.

"Then I need you to come with me right now."

"To where?"

"The packhouse."

*****

Brady 1 hour earlier

No matter how hard I try, I cannot get Shay out of my head. Since the night I kissed her, the only thing Shade wants to do is claim her as ours. He has never wanted another she-wolf as much as he wants her. Because my mom has begun asking too many questions, I am forced to stay away to protect her.

The Alpha ceremony is two nights from now. My plan is to collect Shay, sneak her onto pack lands, hide her in my bedroom, and only after I accept the role as Alpha will I introduce the pack to their new Luna, Shay.

I made up a bullshit story about wanting my invitation hand-delivered to my aunt and uncle; this was the excuse I needed to send Maggie out to buy a dress for our future Luna. I knew my father would never consent to one of our sentinels being sent out on such a menial task. Since my mother made false allegations about Maggie and my relationship, mom has done everything she can to steer clear of Maggie. Allowing her to pick up Shay's outfit.

I have also decided who my Beta will be. I suspect it will be of little surprise to any who knows what Travis did to Shay, yet I also recognize that just like the shock they will soon face realizing Shay will be their leader, I know my father will be blindsided when I announce Colton, not Travis as my Beta.

Not wanting to blindside Colton as much as my desire to confirm this was something he wanted, I accompanied him on his rounds last night. I think he was more surprised that I was making him Beta than what I told him Travis did to Shay. When pressed about it, he quietly confessed when I wasn't around, the way Travis talked about girls, sex, and how he planned to use his title as Beta to make sure they couldn't reject or deny him any of his needs set his teeth on edge while infuriating his wolf. He never told me about his experiences with Travis because he knew Travis and I had been friends much longer than we had.

Needs? After learning just a sliver of what he did to Shay, I can only imagine what those fucking needs might be. How could I have been so utterly blind to the damn monster by my side? No wonder people look at me with fear and disgust filling their eyes.

"What the hell were you thinking, you damnable girl?" My father burst into my office with Natashia hot on his heels.

"But he knew your name, knew our pack name. Hell, he was in Whitefish. How long do you think it would have been before he found us? He told me he had a meeting with you. I didn't think it would be wise to deny an Alpha."

"And how exactly do you know he is an Alpha?" He yells back.

"Does someone want to tell me what the hell is going on?"

"It seems Natashia has gone and invited two males onto our pack lands. One of them is claiming he's the Alpha of another pack."

"Well, where are they?"

"Waiting outside. They refuse to enter the packhouse." Huh, that's odd; whenever you travel to another pack, it is customary to meet the Alpha in his office or in the main room of the pack house. With this guy all but demanding we come out to him, it screams he is the one in charge of this meeting and is dictating the terms of how it will proceed.

"And where the hell is this Alpha from?" I ask while my dad turns to look at Natashia. Evidently, he didn't think to ask her this question.

"Colorado." There is no damn way this could be a coincidence. They have to be here about Shay, but how would they know, and why would they care? Shay told me she had remained rogue. Leaping to my feet, I know I need to be out there standing next to my father if I have any hope of fixing this mess.

By the time Dad and I arrive outside, the entire pack knows about the unwanted visitors, and they have all shown up to find out what they are here for. Striding out onto the porch, I find two men around my age, maybe a few years older, waiting for us. The second my eyes focus on the taller one, I know he is exactly what he claims to be, an Alpha.

"I'm told you wanted to see me." My father's booming voice fills the space. I am not so sure if an entire pack with their Alpha surrounded me, especially one as formidable as my father, that I would stand before him as calm, cool, and collected as this man.

"I do."

"It seems I am at a disadvantage since I don't believe we have ever met."

"Oh, I can assure you we have never met before today. My name is Foster."

"Well.... Alpha," my father spits this word out, fully intending it as the insult it sounded like. "You came all this way. What do you want?"

"I want her back." Fuck. He is here for Shay. I can't let them know she's back before I'm made Alpha. Doesn't this asshole realize how much danger he just put her in?

"Her?"

"Yeah, asshole," this gets my father's attention and not how anyone should want to garner it, "Her."

"I think you're mistaken, young man; we did not take any she-wolf from your pack." My mother attempts to intervene, but this only results in a low growl from his wolf.

"She's here, and you will let me see Shay. Right. Fucking. Now!"

Shit, this just went from bad to a worst-case scenario.

Episode Sixty-Five: Face Off

<u>*Shay*</u>

"ABSOLUTELY NOT. THERE is no way in hell I am going back to the pack."

"Shay—"

"No. I don't know what kind of game you and Brady are playing, but I saw him, so you can drop the damn act." I push past her clearing a path as I storm into the room I've been staying in to pack. It's not surprising when Maggie follows me, slamming the door behind her.

"You knew the Alpha from your pack in Colorado was here, and you didn't think to warn any of us."

"What the hell are you talking about?" I yell as I rip my clothes out of the drawers and throw them into my bag.

"What the hell are *you* talking about?" Maggie snarls while planting her hands on her hips. Looking up at her, I refuse to answer, but so does she. This, ladies and gentlemen, is what we would call a good old-fashioned standoff. Maggie is the first to drop her gaze, so I swallow down my pride and break the silence.

"Travis."

"What?"

"Travis is who I am talking about. So much for the promises you and Brady made me."

"Wait, you saw Travis?"

"Stop lying, Maggie. I'm done playing games. I can't believe I was so damn gullible. No, stupid. Epically monumentally stupid. I have to be the biggest idiot in the world."

"Shay, I promise everything Brady said was true. He is looking for Travis, but it has nothing to do with setting you up. After what Travis did to you, he wants to kill him. He's a good man, and how do you repay his kindness? You don't bother to tell us the Alpha for your new pack would be so pissed off you left with us he'd show up here demanding we turn you over to him."

"What the hell are you talking about? I never joined a Colorado pack and certainly never met their Alpha."

"That's funny because he knows who you are. In fact, he's at the packhouse demanding to see you right now, and based on how he is making demands, I would have to say he isn't too damn happy you left." When I do not move, her demeanor turns from gruff to pleading. "Shay, this is our home, so I am begging you to come back with me."

Relenting, I climb into the car, realizing this could end badly and most likely is the most foolish thing I could do. But my curiosity about who the Alpha is and what he could want with me won out as much as wanting to ensure no one is harmed because of me. Here's hoping he's not in Montana to falsely accuse me of stealing funds, but with the way my luck has been running... it's entirely possible.

Once I arrive on pack land, I will be completely at their mercy. As much as Moon will do everything in her power to protect me, she does not stand a chance against the entire pack. I know she will never be able to withstand being collared again. Furthermore, if she is because I willingly went back to this damn pack, I will never survive knowing I did it to her.

Neither of us said a word to the other for the entire ride back to the one place in the world where I never felt welcome. It's apparent from the lack of conversation that I don't trust her anymore than Maggie believes me.

My heart rate spikes as we pull up, only to discover the entire pack is waiting on us. If I thought the drive back was bad, seeing Tobias, Adela, and Brady on the porch, looking like they were ready to explode, is downright horrifying.

Looking out the back window, I wonder if Moon and I can outrun them. Maybe if I open the door while the car is still moving, shift, and bolt into the woods, I might stand a chance. Deciding this is my best option, I throw the door open, but before I can shift, Tobias's shouts halt my attempt to flee.

"I told you that bitch isn't here."

"Call her a bitch again, old man, and I promise you won't like my response." It can't be him.

"Shay is not going anywhere with you," this has Adela and Tobias bringing their full attention to their son.

"What the hell do you mean, she isn't going anywhere? Do you know where that girl is, Brady?" I noticed Tobias dropped the bitch this time, opting to call me what he always has. Pushing through the crowd, I'm shocked nobody grabs me. My only saving grace is the pack seems so engrossed by what's happening around them no one has any idea I'm the shifter forcing my way past them. This is not to say I am not having any issues because the closer I get to the front of the pack, the more my legs shake, so much so that I am not sure how much longer I will remain upright.

"Shay is coming with me." Pushing past the last line of people, he comes into view, and my heart stops.

Oh, my Goddess, "Foster?"

*****

Brady

"Shay?" the taller one says as he steps toward her. I don't know who this asshole is to her, but if he thinks I am going to let him get any closer, he has another damn thing coming.

"Grab her," mom screams.

"Where's my fucking money, you bitch?" My dad's Beta moves to grab Shay. An act that has the other Alpha, and I guess his Beta, growling as they move closer to her.

"Stay the fuck away from her." "Don't fucking touch her." This guy named Foster and I both yell as we converge on the spot she is standing. Owen stops and looks at my father, who is seething. He's pissed I lied, furious I am protecting her, but he is livid she is back on pack land and still breathing.

"You think you're fucking man enough to keep me away from my mate?"

"Your.... What?" Did he say Shay is his mate? Why the hell didn't she tell me about her mate? Finding your mate is huge. Looking at Shay for answers, she seems horrified. Is she upset he told me this? Is she worried he's here? Is she afraid that I know she lied to me? She keeps telling me she doesn't want to be Luna, but with her mate being an Alpha, how the hell did Shay think she would escape the responsibility this brings?

Two more days. I just needed two more damn days, then I would be Alpha, Shay would be my Luna, and none of the fucking people screaming at her right now would be able to do shit about it. As much as I would like to say Shay chose me, I can tell by the pained look on her face seeing him standing here that it was not so much her choosing me but more her running from him. Now I need to know why she ran. Is he some kind of asshole like Travis? I swear to the Moon Goddess, if he put so much as a fucking finger on her, I will tear him apart.

When one of our sentinels, Pete, moves to grab Shay again, Foster storms in their direction. Before Owen can react, the asshole punches Pete, knocking him flat on his ass, followed by pushing Shay in the direction of the other guy with him. The one I keep assuming is his Beta.

"I told you not to put your fuckin hands on her." I can't say how I know this, but these men don't want to hurt her; they seem.... protective of Shay, and I can make out her quietly asking why they came here.

"Kill him, then bring me that bitch," mom screeches. What the hell is she doing? This guy could have his entire pack surrounding ours right now. Fully prepared to descend the second he signals them to attack. And here my mom is screaming like some damn idiot for someone to kill him. Real damn smart mother. Thank Goddess, dad still has some common sense.

"I am going to give you one minute to turn the thief over to me and get your ass off my land, boy."

"And if I refuse." Foster either has brass balls, his pack backing them up, or he's just fucking crazy.

"If you refuse, I take the goddamn girl, beat the hell out of you, then kick your ass off my fucking lands."

"Is that right? Well, Toby...." Dad's eyes turn deadly hearing him say this. He took it as the insult Foster meant. If this guy wants to make it out of here alive, he better think before he says anything else.

"I challenge you for Pack Alpha." What the fuck did he say?

Episode Sixty-Six: Challenge

Foster

"FOSTER, NO," SHAY screams as she struggles to break free from Finn's hold, but I gave him one very specific order. Protect Shay at all costs. If this goes sideways, he is to get her out of here and back to the truck, where I ordered Ness to remain. I hate pulling the Alpha card with my family, but if it is the only way to keep her ass safely out of the fight and away from danger, she'll have to deal with it.... I'll ask for forgiveness later.

"As his son, I cannot allow you to do this."

"Is that so?"

"Yes."

"Well, as his firstborn son, you don't really have a choice in the fucking matter."

Shay whips her head in my direction while Tobias's face goes ashen and Adela's turns rose red. I hate she found out like this; however, it's out there, and I cannot take it back. Not even for her.

"I would be willing to bet you two fucking assholes never thought you would be face to face with the son you tried to kill. Did you, old man?"

"You are not his son. Tobias has one son, *my* son. You are nothing more than the bastard whelped by the whiny fucking bitch who wasn't good enough to lead this pack."

"And you are nothing more than the whore who hoped to take her place."

"How dare you! I'm the rightful Luna of this pack. The one my husband chose. Tobias didn't want your fucking mother... or you for that matter."

"It seems my dear ol' dad wasn't as over my mom as you had hoped. Since you were already his Luna when he knocked up my mom." Adela's low growl does nothing to stop my tirade.

"Dad?" I don't blame this Brady for his dad's actions. I do blame him for taking my mate, and if he tries to interfere with this shit while I deal with the asshole who broke my mom's heart once and for all, he will regret it.

"I believe I issued you a challenge."

"You cannot come onto our pack lands, challenge my husband for his position and think there will be no ramifications."

"You should keep your bitch on a shorter leash, especially when she doesn't know shit about pack hierarchy," I snap. My eyes narrow on her as my lips twist in a snarl, and my nostrils flare. I have never hated anyone in my entire life, not even my father, and if there was ever a person I should have, it was him. Yet this woman I hate. I hate her for what she did to my mate. I hate her superior attitude. I loathe that after all this time.... She still believes she is better than my mom. I bask in the knowledge that she will soon learn how wrong she is.

"And you should have learned not to insult a better man's wife."

"Show me a better man, and I will give him and his wife respect. What I see is a washed-up old mutt and the bitch who thought she could replace his true mate."

"Foster, don't," Shay screams again. It seems Finn has his hands full with my feisty mate as she battles to break free.

"If you are so sure this is what you want, bastard, then so fuckin be it." Tobias's roar echoes off the trees and buildings. He lumbers down the stairs, his smug-looking wife trailing behind him and one extremely confused-looking, no longer the only son, Brady.

Following Tobias to the ring, I pull my shirt over my head as Shay wiggles out of Finn's grip and runs over to me.

"What are you doing, Foster?"

"Teaching the asshole who killed my mom and hurt my mate there are consequences to his actions."

"How do you know Tobias is your father?"

"When you told me about his mate, I put it all together. I confirmed it with my aunt."

"Are you done playing with the fucking help?" Shadow is clawing wildly to break free; he is as desperate to end this bastard as I am.

"I owe you an explanation, Shay, about everything, but I need to take care of one thing first."

Shay's hands wrap around my wrist. Refusing to release me as her blue eyes blur from unshed tears, while her whispered words caused my heart to ache for her, "Please don't make me witness him kill you too. I don't think I could handle losing someone else I care about in this fucking ring. Please, forget about him, leave me and go home before...."

"I promise I will be back to give you those answers."

"Are you going to continue yammering with the stupid bitch my wife will soon slap a collar on for her role in all this, or will you man the fuck up and prove your worth?"

Nodding for Finch to take Shay away from the ring in case this does not go in my favor, he wraps his arms around her waist and backs through the surging crowd.

I hear his enormous paws before I have the opportunity to shift. Leaping to the side, he smashes into an unfortunate young man, knocking him off his feet. With only seconds to spare before he is on me again, I kick off my pants and phase as I swipe my paw in his direction to knock his snapping muzzle away.

The second I destroy this fucker, kill that bitch too. The demand from Tobias to his Beta is given through their mind link to conceal their plan from me. He doesn't know that I can listen in on their conversation. He's too damn dumb to realize because I am his natural son, I do not need to be his pack mate to hear it.

Shadow has heard enough. We charge at Tobias ramming into his side, which sends him soaring across the ring. Before he can recover, I repeatedly rear up on my hind legs and slam my paws against his already damaged side.

I lunge, hoping to snap my jaws around his neck. If I had accomplished this, it would have ended this fight before it even began, but the asshole is faster than I anticipated, allowing him to twist as he brings his forepaws against Shadow's chest to kick us away. Skidding to a stop, Tobias's wolf was on us while Shadow and I were still regaining our footing. His teeth sink painfully into our shoulder, but Shadow refuses to let him know he hurt us as he swallows down the howl threatening to escape us.

Shay's screams distract us long enough for Tobias to slash his paw out and rip the flesh open on my side. Thinking he has this won, he pounces on my back, but just before he can lock his paws around me, I kick out my back legs and send him tumbling to the ground.

He is only down for a second before we circle one another. He is looking for a weak spot. Shadow and I search for any chink in the armor. Anything we can exploit to end this jackass once and for all.

His wolf is similar in size and strength to Shadow, but I have youth on my side, which grants us something he doesn't have... speed. We are much faster than he or his wolf could hope to be. I whip my paw out, raking my claws over his snout. The howls of pain begin instantly.

"Kill that asshole, baby," Adela screeches from the sidelines. I will enjoy taking her life too.

I meet the deep rumble of his wolf's growl with the same from Shadow. Rearing up on our hind legs, Tobias follows suit. As each of us struggles for dominance, we quickly become nothing but a mass of tangled limbs, snapping jaws, and slashing paws.

But I come out on top, and when he crashes to the ground, with my fangs sunk deep in his throat, he must realize he is not coming out of this circle alive. I can't say if Tobias's next action is born from his understanding that he will soon die or if he thought it would save him. I assure you the latter could not be further from the truth. He does the unthinkable during a challenge; he shifts back to his human form.

"How is your mother, my mate?" The smug quality of his tone has my wolf on the verge of losing all control, but I admit his question surprises me. As such, I feel it merits a response.

Phasing back to my human form, I snap, "You do not get to know anything about my mom. You lost that fucking right the second you rejected her and ordered your Beta to kill her."

"If I had to guess, she is still the weak wolf she always was. Weak, pathetic, useless little Fay."

"Died of a broken fucking heart for a feeble, pitiful old man," he jerks, hoping to drive the blade his Beta tossed to him into my side, but before he can nick my skin, I snap his neck.

And just like that, my useless father, the man who condoned Shay's torment and my mom's heartbreak, is dead.

Episode Sixty-Seven: Renounce

Shay

"NOOOO," ADELA'S SCREAMS fill the air. Foster looks exhausted, Brady seems lost, and I don't know who to comfort first.

"Kill him. Kill the bastard who killed your true Alpha," Adela demands. Several of the male wolves descend on Foster. Before I can break his hold, Finch lifts me off my feet and starts running toward the truck.

"We can't leave him," I yell.

"I'm not, Shay. I just need to get you and Ness out of here first." The hard pants coming from Finn are caused as much by my struggle to break free as they are from him battling his way through the pack, currently surging around my mate.

We have to save them, Shay. Moon's terrified howls rip through me, causing me to jerk in Finn's arms. The sudden action is enough to dislodge me, and the second my feet touch solid ground, I do not waste any time as I sprint back toward Foster.

He seems to have recovered enough to permit him to stand defiant to the wolves rushing him. I push and twist through the shifting crowd, terrified I will not make it to him in time. I am vaguely aware that Finch is yelling my name from somewhere behind me, but Moon's constant whimpers drown out almost everything else.

As I prepare to burst through the swelling pack, Foster's booming voice stops everyone in their tracks.

"As your Alpha, I command you to stand down." And as suddenly as they began swarming him, every shifter stopped and dropped to one knee to acknowledge their new Alpha. With my heart racing, I take the final decisive step past my former pack members to enter the circle where my father met his end. Only to realize my mate and possibly the child he saved has returned years later to confront and end the tyrant who took my parents from me.

"Foster?" He whips around to face me. I truly don't know how I didn't see it before; he is every bit the Alpha he can now call himself. I take a tentative step toward him, but this is as far as I get because Brady comes out of nowhere to yank me back, putting himself between Foster and me.

"Stay the fuck away from her."

"Unless you wish to join your father, you will take your fucking hands off my mate. Right. Now."

"You believe you can come to my pack and order me around? Who the fuck do you think you are?"

"Your Alpha." Foster snaps with enough dominant confidence to send any who remain on both feet to their knees. When Brady does not immediately release me, Foster stalks directly toward us.

"Stop," I yell, jumping between them while Adela screams for Brady to kill me. Of course, she's too stupid to see I am trying to save his life. When Foster hears her order, he does not waste any more time as he rushes forward to pull me away from Brady.

"Foster, Brady, don't." I need them to listen to me. When I realize neither man will allow the other out of the circle, I twist in Foster's arms, putting my back to his chest as I push us further away from Brady. My raised hands finally have Brady looking at me. "Brady, please stop."

"Out of respect for my future Luna, I will honor her request and stop," Brady's hissed response to my pleas has a deep growl rumbling from Foster.

"My mate is already the Luna of this pack. My Luna."

"Okay, first, Shay is no one's Luna," I bark back, knowing if I don't get control of this situation soon, I will lose any hope of stopping these two from a battle to the death.

"Second, if what you say is true and Tobias was your father, it means you two are brothers—"

"I already have a brother. I have no use for this fucker," Foster growls. I know he is referring to Finn; they are as close as any siblings could be.

"You think I give a shit?" Brady barks right back.

Knowing I am losing control, I raise my hands again as I yell, "Third, you are both important to me. You can't hurt each other without destroying me in the process."

Brady's eyes drop from Foster to me, and I can feel Foster's ragged breaths slow slightly. I got their attention. Now I need to convince them not to do what their nature demands. Turning to look at Foster, I quietly tell him, "Brady is a good man. He is nothing like Tobias. He told me about his plans to make the pack better, which is why he asked me to come back with him so I could help him fulfill his promise to his pack. To make life better for everyone, regardless of their position in the pack. Please, Foster, please don't hurt him."

Foster's eyes drop to mine, and in that second.... I know he will do anything I ask of him. Even if I told him that I wanted to stay here with Brady... my mate would accept it. He skims his hand down my cheek, takes one last deep breath, and nods.

"Kill him, son!"

I swear to the Moon Goddess; if Adela doesn't shut her damn mouth, I will wring her fucking neck myself. Knowing if I have any hope of retaining control of the situation here, I spin to face Brady before he can follow through on his mother's demands.

"Brady, I'm sorry."

"For what, Shay?"

"I should have told you I found my mate, and I only agreed to come with you because he didn't want me."

"Then why would you care if I end him?"

"Because even if he doesn't care about me—"

"Let's get one thing perfectly fucking straight here. I never wanted Shay to leave. She is my mate, and I will explain everything to her if she is willing to hear me out." Foster turns me to look at him. "I'm sorry I hurt you, Shay. You deserve the truth, and I promise—"

The sound of Adela screams as she charges through the crowd, knife poised above her head so she can drive it deep into my back has Foster pulling me closer while Brady tackles her.

"What the fuck are you doing, mother?"

"That girl is the reason your father is dead. She needs to pay for what she has done to this pack. I demand you kill her." Brady's eyes narrow. He finally understands Adela would never have accepted me back into this pack. Yanking her up to her feet, he passes Adela over to Colton.

"Put her in the holding cell. I will deal with her later."

"No, she will answer for her actions right here... right now."

"I can't let you do that, man."

"My fuckin name is Foster, not man, and more importantly to you and every other asshole in this pack who ever hurt her, it's Alpha."

"Still, she's my mom."

"And the bitch who ordered my mother's death and beat an innocent girl."

When Brady moves to position himself between Foster and Adela, I know if I don't intercede, Foster will feel like he has no course of action other than to put him down, if only to get to Adela.

"Foster, it's okay. Just let Brady handle her. She's not worth—"

"You're the one not worth the shit on the bottom of my shoes." Adela's screams interrupt my attempt to save her life, making me question why I care if Foster kills her. For a split second, I think about letting him exact a little vengeance on my behalf until Brady's pleading eyes focus on me again. He already lost his dad today. I can't be the reason he loses his mom.

"Foster, please," I repeat, placing my hand against his chest, hoping to pull his attention from the miserable fallen Luna to me.

"Get her out of my damn sight." Brady nods, allowing Colton to pull her towards the pack house again.

"You fucking bitch," she hisses before spitting in my direction.

Foster's fury is palpable, and I can feel his muscles tense. Putting my hands on his face. Instead of attacking her, he merely growls before snapping, "It would serve you well to remember she's the only reason you still draw breath, but I promise if you say another fucking word about Shay, you won't be for long."

"Get her out of here," Brady yells.

"Son, you can't—can't do this to me. I am your mother."

"And right now, mother, you are making everything worse. Besides, you have a lot you will answer for." She screams as Colton pulls her out of the crowd. I remain silent as Brady watches until Colt vanishes through the door before slowly turning to face us again. "So you want to be the Alpha of this pack?"

Foster doesn't respond; instead, he stares at Brady, waiting to hear what he plans to say.

"My dad or I guess if what you say is correct, our dad—"

"That fucker was never my dad."

"Fair enough, Tobias was not a good Alpha. His choices over the years hurt this pack and members within it." His eyes flick to me. "Shay and every other wolf in this pack deserve a better life than they had when he was in charge. I wanted to make those changes, but if Shay trusts you, I will too."

"Does anyone wish to challenge me for the role of Alpha?" Foster shouts. When no one accepts, he continues.

"No? Good. Then I renounce my right as Alpha of the Half Crest Moon pack. Maybe you can do what he couldn't, but remember, if I find out, you are just a younger version of that asshole." Foster walks closer to Brady, so only the three of us can hear him. "I will be back."

Episode Sixty-Eight: Goodbyes

Brady

HOW DID I go from planning an Alpha ceremony where I intended to announce Shay as my chosen Luna to my dad, being dead at my feet by the brother I never knew I had? And worse, all while Shay is preparing to leave with him.

Like an idiot, I stood there silent instead of trying to convince her to stay with me here in Whitefish as he repeatedly begged her to return to Lake with him. He assured her it was her home now, even if she didn't want anything to do with him. He and his pack would always protect her, and unlike what she faced here, they would welcome her if she ever decided she wanted to be a part of a pack again.

It was not until his Beta chimed in about how they needed their champ back home to keep putting him; I assume '*the him*' is Foster, in his place every Tuesday, that she finally smiled. I don't think I need to tell you how much it hurt my heart when she agreed to return with them.

At least he walked away so I could tell her goodbye without him growling every two seconds.

"Well, I guess I understand why you kept bringing up the whole mate thing now."

"I'm sorry, Brady. I never...."

"Shay, you don't owe me an apology. In fact, you don't owe anybody anything. Not me, not this pack, not him." I do my best to contain my disdain for her mate when I say this last part as I flick my head toward the guy she will soon leave with. "The only thing you need to do is find what will at long last give you any amount of pleasure. I would be the happiest man in the world if it were here with me. If your happiness lies in Lake with him, then I will find contentment knowing you are right where you want to be, or if it is someplace else, I will do everything I can to help you find it and settle in. The bottom line is, I want you to be happy, Shay."

"Thank you, Brady. I meant what I said; you are a good man, and I genuinely believe you will be a good Alpha. I don't know if what I am about to say will make any difference. If it will help or hurt, but I feel like I need to tell you regardless." She takes a deep breath before placing her hand against my chest.

"If I had never met Foster, I would have been happy here with you, with the changes I know you will make, and I don't know if Foster and I will end up together, but I do know you should at least try to find your mate because you deserve it." She gently kisses my cheek, but I have other plans as I grab her to smash my lips to hers. If this is the last time I will ever get to kiss her, I want her to remember it, to remember me. I'll admit the rush of excitement I feel when she does not instantly pull away from me is indescribable, but the satisfaction I get hearing him growl when he sees us is almost as gratifying.

When she pulls away, I wink before telling her, "If he doesn't treat you right or if you change your mind, I want you to know you always have a place here with me, Shay."

Moving my eyes over to the asshole who will soon whisk away the woman I had planned on marrying, I can't help but feel a twinge of jealousy flare to life again. I wonder if he knows what a rare and wonderful woman he has. With Shay still hugged to my chest, I hope he understands I will hunt him down if he ever hurts her.

Foster's eyes remained glued to my interaction with Shay; if looks could kill, I may be dead in her arms. It seems my yet-to-be-determined brother doesn't care to share. Although when it comes to Shay, I can't say I blame him. I wouldn't be so keen to allow another to hug her if she were mine, either.

Speaking of the yet-to-be-determined part, I plan on discussing this with my mother post haste. If this is true, it means not only did my father agree to kill his own son, but it also indicates my mother ordered it. I don't understand how she could do something so cold, so I need her to explain what happened.

Shay pulling out of my embrace leaves an emptiness I am unaccustomed to experiencing. I suddenly realized what a complete and utter tool I've been all these years when I gave women any ray of false hope we may be together. Not that I ever promised anyone anything, but Shay never promised me anything either, and I am left wishing things could have been different. I suddenly feel like I owe them all a huge apology.

"I better get going. We have a long drive ahead of us."

"Listen, Shay, just remember, even though you are returning with them doesn't mean you owe him anything. If he cares about you as he claims to, he will allow you to decide what you want."

"Thank you, Brady."

"For what?"

"Caring enough to make things better. Will you keep in touch?"

"Nothing could ever keep you from me."

"Shay?" I look up to see Nan tentatively walking toward us.

"Nan." Shay rushes over, pulling her into her arms. Hugging her more fiercely than I have ever seen before. Nan's eyes are filled with tears as she strokes Shay's hair.

"Oh, my sweet girl, I never thought I would see you again." "I missed you terribly." Nan and Shay say in unison as they continue to cling to each other. I knew Nan missed her, but it was not until this moment I realized how much. And it seems Nan's feelings were not one-sided.

Foster's slow approach confirms my time alone with Shay is done.

"This must be Nan?" He asks as he places his hand on Shay's back. I can feel Shade stir; it seems he is just as jealous as I am.

"I am, and who may I ask are you, young man?"

"My name is Foster. I'm...." He hesitates to look at Shay for permission. His eyes desperately hoping she will grant it to him, and suddenly I know he cares about her every bit as much as I do, perhaps more. Shay smiles at him before looking at Nan.

"He's my mate."

Nan's beaming smile confirms the news thrilled her. I wonder if she would have been as happy with me marrying Shay as she appears to be looking at Foster. He respectfully presents his hand to her, which Nan graciously accepts.

"Are you home for good?" Shay's face drops as sadness replaces the beaming smile she wore just seconds ago.

"No, Nan. I have a new home in Colorado." She looks up at Foster before asking in a questioning manner, "A new pack?"

"A pack who is fortunate to have her." He confirms as he places his hand against the back of her neck, giving him access to run his thumb across her cheek, causing another wave of jealousy to course through me.

"Oh." Nan's previous elation is quickly replaced with dejection.

"Why don't you come with us, Nan?" Shay asks, and my initial reaction is to deny Shay's request, but when I see her hopeful expression as she looks first at Foster, who seems overjoyed at the prospect, how can I be the one to deny either of them what they really want?

So when Nan looks at me next, I gently place my hand on her shoulder before I tell her, "Nan, your place is where you want it to be. You will always be welcome here, but if you want to go with Shay, you have my blessing."

I was unprepared for the hug Nan gave me, but I knew I had done the right thing when she did. I guess this is what it means to be a good Alpha, not doing what is best for you, but what is best for the members of your pack.

Fifteen minutes later, I watch as the shifter, I believe they called Finn escorts Nan toward their waiting truck. I can only hope I am making the right call as I give Shay one last hug. He does seem to care about her, and I already told her she could come back anytime. The next thing I do is one of the hardest things I have ever done. I offer my hand to Foster.

"Take care of them," I say as I wait to see if he will accept my offered hand.

"With my life," he confirms as he extends his hand to meet mine. After this, he leads Shay away from the home I had hoped would be her salvation. As I watch her go, one thing continues to twist my thoughts: my mother has a lot of explaining to do.

Episode Sixty-Nine: Without

Shay

I ADMIT TO being slightly overwhelmed. This morning I started the day slated to be the Luna of the Half Crest Moon pack, and now I am traveling back to Colorado with Nan but even crazier with the mate I didn't think wanted me.

When I arrived back at the truck, I was shocked to find Ness waiting for us. She and Nan were already sitting in the back seat while Finn was standing outside, arm resting on the open passenger door. When I started to climb into the back seat, Foss grabbed my hand to stop me as Finn climbed back there instead.

Sitting next to Foster, I let my eyes settle for what may be the last time on my previous pack, but more importantly, Brady, who lifts his hand to wave as Foster backs out. Seeing him fade away in the side mirror, I cannot help but feel a slight twinge of loss. I won't miss the pack; however, I will miss him and Maggie.

An hour into our return trip, neither Foster nor I have said a word, but Nan and Ness more than make up for the silence.

Ness has already taken to Nan, and they are chatting about the old fashion apple muffins Nan loves to make. Even Finn chimes in with an oooh, yum, and how soon do you plan on making these. As minutes drift into hours and the silence between Foster and me continues, I am beginning to question if I made the right decision.

I know he promised me he would tell me everything, and having that conversation in a car full of other people is probably not the right time to do it, but with every mile that passes, I can't help but feel like the distance between us is growing.

"Are you all okay if we get a couple of rooms in the next town? I could use some rest." Foster's question may be something he is asking everyone, but his side-eyed glances are solely on me. I guess I never thought about how tired he must be from the fight, and if I'm not mistaken, he was injured during the challenge. Shadow will help him heal, but rest is what he needs most.

The overall sentiment is one of agreement. After finding a motel and getting four rooms, Foster retires to his while the rest of us go to get something to eat. The conversation is light, yet I cannot help my thoughts as they continually return to Foster.

"It's okay if you want to check on him," Finn quietly tells me as he leans closer.

"No, he said he wanted to rest, so I should—"

"Nonsense, child, that boy's eyes never left you the entire time he was talking," Nan interrupts.

"Yeah, Shay, I don't think Foster made those comments to keep *you* away," Ness giggles. "In fact, spending some time with you may be just what the doctor ordered, and as a Salutary, I know these kinds of things."

"I shouldn't leave Nan alone since tonight is the first night she has ever been away from the—"

"Pish posh, now don't you use me as an excuse to stay away from the handsome young man waiting for you back at the hotel."

"I guess I could order him something to eat," as if expecting I was going to say this, the waitress brings a bag of food over to the table.

"Well, look at that. Food for our Alpha," Finn says as he winks at the waitress, who returns his grin with one of her own.

Waiting until she walks away, I quietly correct, "Foster is not an Alpha. He gave up the position."

"Tsk, Tsk, Shay," Finn says, waving a finger at me, "Don't you try to get information out of us. Now, shoo."

Picking up the bag, I look at them over my shoulder before deciding it is time for me to find out what the hell is going on.

"Oh, and Shay."

"Yes?" I say, looking back at Finn.

"Go easy on him." His smirk indicates he means more than just during our talk.

Rolling my eyes, I hear Ness groan before saying, "Yuck, Finch."

"What? My brother had an exhausting day; he could use a little Shay attention to help him feel better. Sorry, Nan."

Nan's comment is more shocking than Finn's but has Ness bursting out laughing hysterically while my face turns bright red. "I'm old, son, not dead."

By the time I return to the motel, all my confidence after leaving the diner has melted away. Standing outside the door to Foster's room, I contemplate sitting the bag on the ground, knocking twice before hustling back to the room I am sharing with Nan.

Cowardly? Yes. What is probably going to happen? Definitely.

With the bag situated where he will not miss it, I knock twice and turn to leave, but I only make it a couple of steps when he opens the door.

"How was your dinner?"

"I didn't mean to... I mean... It was fine. How are you feeling?"

"Fine," he says with a smirk as he mimics my tone. "Did everyone else turn in for the night already?"

"No, they're still at the diner. I thought maybe.... I wanted.... You know what? It doesn't matter. Enjoy your food."

"Shay, can we talk?" He asks as he steps back, leaving enough space for me to enter the room.

"You should probably get some rest."

"I'll rest later. Right now I would like to spend some time with you so I can.... I owe you an explanation. Besides, I hate eating alone," he says, picking up the bag.

I hesitate, but when he tilts his head toward his room, I relent and follow him inside. Once we are seated at his table, he pushes the food aside, taking my hands in his.

"First, I owe you an apology for leaving like I did the night we were at your place."

"Why did you?"

"Because I had to find out if my mom and I were the reason you lost your parents."

"You think that would have made a difference to me?"

"It mattered to me, Shay. How could I possibly look you in the eyes, knowing your life was stolen so I could have one?"

"Because you matter to me, Foster. Do you think I would have been any happier knowing my dad killed a woman heavy with her pup?"

"No, because you have a good heart, yet I still felt unworthy of you."

"Well, you shouldn't. You didn't ask my dad to do it. He did it because he was a good man like you. If I'm being honest, I love my dad even more, knowing he saved the baby who would one day be his daughter's mate."

"But the question remains.... Is his daughter still willing to accept him as her mate?"

"Why did you tell everyone you were an Alpha before you killed Tobias?"

Foster clears his throat before saying something I am unprepared for, "Because I am."

"You are what?"

"An Alpha. I am the Alpha of Ash Rock."

"Why didn't you ever tell me?"

"Because you left before I could."

"You didn't think to say anything before we spent the night together?"

"I hadn't become the Alpha until after that night. I planned on telling you everything before releasing my bond to you, but you left with...." he clears his throat, gritting his teeth as he finishes with, "Brady."

"So you want to break our bond?"

"No, but I figured you would after I told you about your dad."

"Are you sure you don't want to break our bond?" Foster stands, hauling me to my feet and into his arms.

"Never, Shay. I would sooner pull my heart from my chest than have my bond with you broken." My heart soars, knowing my feelings for him are not as one-sided as I had thought. In my elation, I tighten my hold on him, resulting in a wince from him.

"Oh Goddess, you're still hurt?"

"Yeah, he got me pretty good."

"I should let you rest."

"Being here with you is all the rest I need."

"Well, let me at least look at it."

"If you want me to take my shirt off, beautiful, you just need to ask."

Shaking my head, I cross my arms over my chest as I say, "I want to see how bad it is so I know if I need to get Ness to look at it."

"Yeah, just so you know, I don't need my cousin tonight. You, on the other hand...." He leans down, brushing his lips over mine.

"I can't live without."

Episode Seventy: Tell Me

Shay

HIS LIPS ON mine send a thrill rushing through me as every nerve in my body goes haywire, and it's not just me who can feel it. Moon is soaring high from being this close to Shadow.

"I never thought I would ever get the chance to do this again," he pulls me tighter into his embrace. "Worried I had lost you after just finding you."

We have been backing slowly toward his bed the entire time he was talking. When my legs strike against the mattress, he pulls back, showing me a wicked but sexy-as-hell grin covering his face.

"I really should go. You need to rest so you can heal."

He nods before he kisses my jaw and neck, but when he pulls my earlobe into his mouth, biting it gently, my knees almost buckle.

"Tell me what you really want, Shay?"

"I — I," as much as I want to tell him what I want, the words refuse to take form. Right now, the only thing I can think about is his lips on my skin, the warmth of his breath on my neck, and the husky baritone of his voice.

"Use your words, beautiful."

"Should go," I finally manage to finish.

"Are you sure about that?" He asks, sliding his hands down to my waist so he can grasp the bottom of my shirt. When I shake my head, he grins but will not relent. "Words, sweetheart, use your words."

"No, I want...."

He presses his lips to mine, sliding his tongue over them. "Want what?"

"You," I moan as he sucks my lower lip into his mouth.

"Lie back."

"You're hurt. We should wait—"

"I said to lie back," he tells me, pulling my shirt over my head. "Because I fully intend on hearing you scream my name tonight."

Heat coils through my body until it lands firmly between my thighs. My pulse pounds as Foster slowly begins sliding my pants down, following their path with his very skilled mouth. A nip here, a lick there, followed by a bite to the inside of my thigh, and I could not stop the moan from rushing out of me even if I tried.

His fingertips skim over the lace of my panties. I quiver as my stomach jumps. Tightness clenches every muscle in my body from the sheer anticipation of him touching me. He kisses my stomach as his fingers wrap around the lacy sides. At a painfully slow pace, he slides them down, kissing every newly exposed inch of skin as he goes.

"Lie. Down."

He moves further between my legs when I remain upright, close enough to allow his tongue to run over my clit. The dampness which has been building this whole time explodes, coating the insides of my thighs. My hands twist in his hair as I attempt to pull away from him, but he refuses to allow my retreat.

"You can either lie back or risk your legs giving out as I continue to feast on you, beautiful." His arms snake around my thighs, hands kneading my ass, pulling me closer as his tongue continues its blissful ministrations.

I stop pulling away and instead pull him closer. My every thought shifts to releasing the building climax, now begging to explode. His skilled tongue helps me chase the pleasure he seems so willing to provide.

When he tires of the angle not allowing him the access he wants, he grabs my arms and pulls until I crash against the bed. Not one to waste time, he repositions us to give himself full access to me. He kisses the inside of each thigh before running his tongue back over the folds, now soaked from his attention as much as my excitement.

With his unobstructed position, he is pushing me closer to the heavenly brink of my orgasm. Every muscle in my body is coiled tight with each teasing flick of his tongue against my clit. I'm so close; just a few more sweeps. Just.... Another.... Flick.

Foster pulls away, taking his magical tongue with him, refusing to give me what I want, what I need.

"Tell me what you want. I want to hear you say it."

"Please, Foster."

"Please, what?"

"Please don't stop."

"Tell me what you want," he demands with a growl.

"I want to come." My response comes out as a begging whimper. I don't care if I sound pathetic; he has me so turned on right now it is damn near painful.

"How?"

"I don't understand your damn question," I pant.

"How do you want me to make you come? With my hand, my cock, or my tongue. Tell me. I want to hear you say it, and then I will give you what you want."

"Foster, please."

"Say the words, Shay." He repeats as he slides the shirt over his head before dropping his pants. My eyes focus on his massive erection, and I remember how wonderful it felt having him drive in and out of me. The walls of my pussy clamp at the thought of him slamming inside me.

His hand grabs his hard length. I admit I'm slightly jealous seeing him slide his hand up and down. Each and every stroke further confirms that I want to be the one doing this to him. Precum glistens at the tip of his erection, and I have the overwhelming desire to run my tongue along it.

I reach between my legs, figuring if he refuses to take care of this burning ache, I'll do it myself, but he knocks my hand away.

"Ahhh—ah, Shay, you only get to come when you tell me how you want to do it, and I promise you, sweetheart, your hand is not one of the options."

"Foster," I growl. Now he's just pissing me off.

"Tell me, and I'll grant you anything you want."

Not wanting to give in to him, I glare at the man who seems to enjoy torturing me as I prop myself up on my elbows. Crossing my legs doesn't help much because now I don't just have a burning ache but a pulsing burning ache. Fuck my life right now.

If he wants to play games, then so can I.

"Nah, I'm kind of enjoying watching you."

His eyes light up, blazing from his desire, yet I admit his grin is damn near my undoing.

"So be it, my little vixen."

His hand slides faster, his breath ragged. I watch as he glides his tongue over his lips.

"Mmmm, I can still taste you on my lips. I wonder, can you still feel my tongue against your clit?"

Oh, he does not fight fair. Squeezing my thighs together tighter does nothing to abate the memory of his tongue sliding over me. His hand on my leg has me believing he will finally give in, but he merely separates my legs so he can see me dripping wet and waiting for him to fill me.

"I'm getting closer, Shay. Are you sure this is how you want this to play out?" Every stroke makes the deep baritone in his tone richer.

Breath caught in my throat, pulse pounding in my ears and between my soaked thighs. We hold each other's gaze until I know I have no hopes of winning this.

"Your tongue." One extremely triumphant grin replaces his wicked smile.

Is it possible to hate someone and love them at the same time?

Episode Seventy-One: Mine

Foster

WHEN SHE FINALLY told me what she wanted, I was happy to oblige. I was on the brink of giving in, especially when her eyes followed every stroke of my hand around my dick. I didn't lie when I told her the taste of her still lingered on my lips, and now as I drop down to take my position between her silky thighs, I wish she would have said cock.

No matter because after I give her what she asked for, I plan on sliding inside her to finish what I started.

With every sweep of my tongue, she raises her hips, begging for more. Sliding my hands up her stomach until I find those perfect breasts, I graze one thumb over her erect nipple, and the moan she gives me confirms she wants more.

I have never wanted to hear the sounds she gives me so much in all my life. I could live and die by those sexy fucking sounds alone.

Shadow would like nothing more than for us to mark her, declaring she is ours to the entire world, but this will only happen if she consents. For far too long, her choices were never considered. What she wanted didn't matter, but moving forward, it will all be for her to decide. From how we do it, when it happens, or if she even agrees to let me make love to her are all things I will not take from her.

"Foster," she moans, pulling my head closer against her, and I know she is so close to stepping off so she can tumble into the abyss of her climax, and the thought has my dick stiffening painfully.

Watching her masturbate was very tempting, but Shay was wound so tight I knew if she touched herself, she would come before making her choice known. Besides, I wanted to be the one to make her moan. I wanted it to be my tongue running against her engorged clit, not her fingers.

She stifles a scream by pressing her forearm against her mouth while the high she has been chasing crashes over her. I hate she feels the need to do this. I want to hear every moan, every groan, every fucking scream she wants to give me. The second we return to Lake, I plan on kicking everyone out of my fucking cottage so I can pleasure her until I hear them all, and I will only allow her to come if she promises not to restrain any of them.

Lapping up every delicious drop, she groans, trying to push me away every time my tongue brushes against her hyper-sensitive clit.

"Foster," she moans as she wiggles to separate my mouth from her pussy.

Kissing my way up her stomach, I brush my lips, still wet from her orgasm, over her nipple. Her hand knots in my hair, encouraging me to take one into my mouth. She meets the growl rumbling through me with one of her own.

Not one to disappoint such an exceptional beauty, I suck one between my teeth as my fingers rub across the other.

"I'm going to fuck you until you beg me to stop, Shay."

"Yes."

"Tell me to fuck you. Tell me how much you want to feel me filling you up. Ramming inside you, taking you over and over."

"Please."

"Please, this word doesn't tell me shit, Shay. In fact, unless I tell you to say it from now on, I will stop every time you use this worthless word instead of what you want to say. Besides, my sexy mate, you don't beg for anything."

"I want you to fuck me," she tells me with a breathy demand.

"With what?"

"Your cock. I want to feel you inside me until I scream your name." With her next choice made, she smashes her mouth to mine. Her tongue darts hungrily between my parted lips, massaging it against mine. A low moan escapes her as she tastes herself there.

I don't slide slowly inside her; I slam into the warm, wet folds of the sweetest thing I have ever experienced.

She frantically claws at my back, pain and pleasure, pleasure and pain. They are two sides of the same coin. She gives me both, and I admit I like it far more than I thought possible, but then again, it could be the woman providing them more than the sensation itself.

I tear my lips away from hers to roll us over, putting Shay on top and fully in control of our pleasure. I'm sure she thinks this is another way for me to demand how this will go, but it couldn't be further from the truth.

"Tell me, Shay, did it turn you on, watching my hand sliding up and down on my dick?"

She rolls her hips, making me groan before she replies, "As much as watching you between my legs."

Fucking hell. I didn't think I could be any more turned on, but she just sent me soaring from merely being turned on straight to the edge of losing my fucking mind. Dragging her hips against me, she bites down on that perfect lip still swollen from our kiss.

I want to bite that lip too. In fact.... Sitting up, I first stop to suck a nipple into my mouth, applying gentle pressure from my teeth, which causes her to throw her head back. Moving to the other side produces another moan as she grinds on my dick harder. Faster. Sending me spiraling toward my orgasm.

Flipping her onto her back, I drill into her at a frantic pace. The lip I wanted to bite now held firmly between my teeth.

"Mine."

"Yours," her confirmation sends a rush of pleasure through my entire body.

I feel her tighten around me, signaling she is on the brink. Not wanting her to hold back, I smash my mouth against hers to swallow up the moan she was trying so hard to suppress. She brings her legs up, tucking them between my arms and chest. Huh, she has learned fast. This is a position I definitely approve of.

The force of my climax has me spilling every drop inside her as I moan out her name this time.

Afterward, we lay tangled in each other's arms. The pain in my side returns for the first time since I kissed her. Fuck, he got me good. The damage will probably take a couple of days to fully heal.

Suck it up, Sally. She is worth every ounce of pain. Shadow growls.

I never said she wasn't, furball. I snap back.

Damn right, and the best part is.... No more blue balls.

I want to argue, but I don't because I would rather concentrate on my gorgeous mate and because he's not wrong. And let's face it, I would rather admit to anything but that.

Episode Seventy-Two: So It Begins

Brady

IT HAS BEEN a little over a month since Foster showed up, killed my dad, threatened to kill my mom, claimed and then passed the title of Alpha over to me, and took the woman I thought I would spend the rest of my life with back to Colorado.

I have to admit I held out hope she would change her mind. Right up until the last sliver of his taillights disappeared down the road. It was only then I understood she was never mine to marry.

It doesn't take the sting away or the realization that I will probably never see her again.

Maggie and Colton have become invaluable to me as I work to reverse all the damage my parents did to this pack over the years. I also don't miss their stolen glances at each other. Last night I told him to quit being an idiot and ask her out. Here's hoping he'll take my advice.

Natashia has made herself noticeably scarce lately. I figure all the changes I am putting into place don't sit well with her, but more likely, she is just trying to avoid having an assignment given to her. She still believes she is some kind of ruler and above menial work.

I hate to break it to Natashia, but she's wrong. No one, not even me, is above working to get this pack running smoothly.

Most of the other shifters have embraced the changes I am making. The ones who didn't were free to leave. I swore no harm would come to them, a promise I upheld even when others counseled me otherwise.

I can't preach change while holding onto old beliefs.

The first to leave was my dad's beta, Owen. I didn't figure he would stick around, although I had hoped. I would have listened to his advice; after all, he had years of experience running this pack and keeping it thriving. I guess I should clarify I would have been open to hearing what he had to say, provided it did not center on anyone's position within this pack or how we treated them.

When he didn't leave right away, I figured he might stay, but after we had a heated argument two weeks ago about how to handle mom and Foster, he left. He thought we should take the fight to Foster to exact our revenge for killing my dad. I disagreed.

My mother is a whole other issue altogether. I am not sure what to do about her. She has made it abundantly clear she has no intention of falling in line with the direction I want to take the pack. Not to mention I always have it in the back of my head that Foster may return.

I don't fear facing him, but I am not a stupid man. My father was an experienced warrior who fell by Foster's hand.

"What are you up to, Brady?" Colton's greeting pulls my attention from the paperwork I wasn't truly concerned about to begin with.

"Hey, Colt. How is everything going?"

"Surprisingly well. Most of the pack is adjusting nicely to the changes."

"This is the first bit of good news I've heard today. Have we lost anyone else?" Even though I said we haven't lost many of the pack members, this fear is something I imagine will linger in the back of my head for months to come.

"Only one—"

"What the fuck happened here?" Okay, this is the one meeting I have been dreading the most. Having to face my uncle and inform him his brother is dead. I didn't want to outright lie to him; I just needed to get things situated here first. I should have figured Owen would run straight to him after he left.

"Where's Tobias?"

"Uncle Sebastian, please sit down."

"I don't fucking need to sit down, boy. I need you to tell me the bullshit his Beta told me is just that bullshit."

"I'm sorry I wanted—"

"Wanted to what? Tell me my only brother was killed by some miserable little prick claiming to be his son. The same little prick who only came here because you wanted to claim his mate as your Luna when your father handed you this pack. An Insignificant bitch, this pack sheltered her whole life. The same little bitch my brother allowed to keep her pathetic life even after her traitorous bastard father challenged him for his position. Is this what you wanted to tell me, nephew?"

I understand his fury. He just found out his brother is dead. This doesn't mean I can allow him to storm in here and treat me any differently than he would any other Alpha. Abruptly standing, the chair I was sitting in slams against the wall as a low growl rumbles through my chest.

"Uncle, I get that you're fucking pissed, but you will keep in mind that I am the Alpha here, not you. As such, you will show me the damn respect I deserve."

"Respect. You want to talk to me about respect. Your dad, my brother, was killed over a fucking month ago, and I only found out because his Beta told me. Because of your decisions, neither your grandfather nor I were permitted to say goodbye. And worse, I hear you let the fucker who did this shit saunter out of here with the little bitch who caused this entire cluster fuck."

"You will not speak about Shay like—" Before I finish my sentence, my uncle catches me off guard when he charges at me, slamming me back into the wall. His forearm pushed painfully against my throat, making it damn near impossible to take my next breath.

"I will talk about that little bitch however I want." I can't believe his next action when he punches me. The impact of the hit sends my head snapping to the side.

I admit I never thought he would do something like this to me. I have always been close to my uncle. Even during the times I couldn't talk to my dad, he was there to guide me. I think this is what makes the assault hurt the most. Not the physical part, the emotional part.

This does not mean I will allow this to stand. I twist my arm to dislodge his before returning a blow of my own. The hit delivers the desired effect as my uncle stumbles away, rubbing his jaw.

"No, you fucking won't." My breaths are coming in ragged pants. I stand tall, feeling like the Alpha I am for the first time. "I apologize you missed his memorial, but had my father not done some of the shit he did, none of this would have happened."

"Bullshit—" I refuse to allow him to overrule me anymore.

"You can say bullshit all you like, but the facts are clear. Had my father never sent his Beta to kill his mate, Shay's dad would not have had to disobey his Alpha. Foster may have had a father, and Shay would have had parents and not been treated like a servant in her own fucking pack. All of these were decisions my father, your fucking brother, as well as my mother made. Decisions directly responsible for his death. Not Shay. So you will show her the respect she fucking deserves when you are on my pack's lands. Do I make myself perfectly fucking clear?"

"And I suppose the bastard who killed my brother will not have to face justice."

"My brother has returned to his pack, and I can assure you I have no intention of doing anything to him."

"Your brother? Your brother!" His snarled response confirms he does not agree with me referring to Foster as my brother.

"Yes. My brother. What fucking part of these two words did you not understand?" I growl. My fury at having someone question my decisions, even if it is my uncle, is pissing me off.

"If this is how you feel, Alpha," he spits the word out to show he does not agree with the title. "Don't call upon my pack for anything ever again. The bond between our packs is over. You're on your own, *Brady*."

"I never said I needed your pack, *Sebastian*."

"I want the Luna of this pack turned over to me."

"This pack currently does not have a Luna," I snap right back.

"You will give me my brother's widow."

"My mother will remain right where the fuck she is until I decide what will happen to her."

"You will regret your choices."

"Well then, I guess it's good that you won't be around to worry about it." My uncle's glare confirms any bond we had is gone. I remain silent as he turns to stalk out of the room. Looking at two sentinels for my pack, I nod for them to follow him. I want to ensure he vacates my lands.

"I get the distinct feeling this is not over yet, Brady," Colton cautiously declares.

"Agreed. We need to increase the patrols, and daily training sessions should begin again."

I guess this is what it means to be on my own.

Episode Seventy-Three: Shhh

Shay

AFTER WE RETURNED to Lake, I asked Foster to keep things between us quiet for a while. I thought we needed time to figure out where this was going before we took anything public. Not to mention being involved with an Alpha was certainly never something I expected to happen to me.

Besides, Foster needs time to settle into his new role. He still hates the idea of leading, but given the opportunity, I believe he will make a great one.

Thankfully, Seamus gave me my job and the house back. Foster wanted me to live with him at the cottage; when I refused, he asked me to move onto pack lands. Again I declined. I admit being a part of a pack again will take time to get used to. And a lot of trust. Which, let's face it, is not something I have an abundance of. But with Nan settling in so easily, I admit the thought is growing on me.

"Bollocks," Seamus shouts from the kitchen as a loud crash confirms he broke another stack of plates. I do not know what's got him so rattled since I returned, but something is off.

"Seamus," I say cautiously as I push the door open. "Is everything alright in here?"

"Not a titter of wit, that one," he grumbles.

"I'm not sure who you're talking about."

"Does me head in, chasing that bloody chancer around like the sun rises and sets on his arse." He yells as he turns to look at me.

"Still not sure who we're talking about."

"Me niece, Riona."

"I assume this is about a guy?"

"Aye, she either wants what she can't have or chases what she shouldn't want."

"How old is she?"

"Twenty for another month then, Ms. Big Breeches will be all grown up and giving me even more headaches. Not a twitter of wit. Egit'."

"Let me guess, she doesn't care for people telling her what to do."

"Aye, and now me sister is sending her here before she can run off with the bloody chancer."

"Here? As in here in America or here as in Lake?"

"Aye, here. Me sister's headache will soon be my new pain in the arse."

"She can't be that—" Before I can finish, he returns to yelling stuff in Irish, things I don't have a hope in hell of understanding. The rant continues for several minutes, with me standing there waiting for him to finish.

"Bollocks."

"Okay, I'll just get back to work then." His mumbled Irishisms continue, making me grin as I walk out.

"Is our red-headed friend still melting down about his niece's pending arrival?" Hyde asks.

"It would seem so," I confirm, cracking a new beer for him before I get another one for Jerry.

"You, my lovely," hiccup, "are a god…. Godsend. Don't leave us a—" hiccup, "again."

"No worries, Jer, because I'm here to stay."

I spent the next couple of hours preparing the bar for the influx of people we will have here tonight for the tournament. Mandy is still avoiding me. We keep our conversations to excuse me when we try to pass each other behind the bar; can you grab that one when one of us needs to use the restroom. And Mandy's personal favorite: you can do stock tonight; I have plans. Of course, these plans are always centered around her flirting with Foster. Which is not fucking okay with me.

Ness keeps telling me I don't have anything to worry about, but let's face it, I haven't had the best luck thus far, so here's hoping she's right.

The second Foster and Finch come in, the single women in the bar all let out collective sighs. A month of this shit, and I'm still not used to it. I admit the sexy grin he flashes me; at least it better be for me, has my heart ramping up.

As soon as she sees me heading over to his table, Mandy yells, "Cover my section. I need to take table orders."

Of course she does. Opening the cooler to get another beer for Hyde, I realize Mandy never filled it. Great, just great. Waiting until Mandy saunters her ass back behind the bar, I storm into the stockroom to grab our missing supplies.

I have cases of beer stacked halfway up the dolly when the closing door has me sighing my frustration.

"I'm almost done, Mandy. It wouldn't be an issue if you stocked the damn coolers on your side," I snap before spinning, only to find Foster standing there.

"Good to know, but not Mandy."

"Foss, what are you doing in here?"

"You didn't stop by last night."

"I didn't get out of here until late, and I didn't want to wake you."

Foster locks the door before he ambles over toward me. The look in his eye is akin to a hungry lion stalking his prey, and the sight sends a rush of excitement coursing through me. His hands on my face and lips against mine do nothing to extinguish the building flame.

"Let's get one thing straight, beautiful." He kisses my neck before he skims his lips back up to mine. "You can always wake me."

He trails kisses down my jaw, across my clavicle, to the top of each breast, over my stomach, straight to…. "Holy mother and Mary."

"Shhh. Unless you want the entire bar to hear you, sweetheart."

"Foster, I'm at work."

"Don't let me stop you." The husky, deep, sultry timbre from his comment sends a jolt through me and straight between my legs. The legs he is currently nestled between. Kissing me in places he shouldn't be kissing, at least not while I'm at work.

"Foster," I moan, knotting my hands in his hair.

"Beautiful, I could care less if the entire bar hears me pleasing you, but if you don't want people to hear you, I suggest you control those sexy little sounds you're making." He grins up at me, forcing me to shove the side of my hand in my mouth to stifle the next moan building there.

That goddamn skilled tongue of his has me panting in seconds, but just before I reach the peak, he stands up, pulls his pants down, and wraps my legs around his waist. He slowly pushes inside me, claiming my lips and swallowing the moan he is causing.

The doorknob jiggles, threatening to expose us in an extremely compromising position. I try to pull away from Foster, but he refuses to release me, opting to continue with his slow sensual thrust.

"Shay, are you still in there?" I groan as much from hearing Mandy's voice as having his mouth claiming my nipple.

"Fuck," I hiss.

He kisses me but shows no signs of stopping. "You plan on answering her, sweetheart."

"Yeah." my first attempt is breathier than I intended. Which makes Foster chuckle.

"You might want to try that again, baby doll."

Clearing my throat, my second attempt is much more believable. "I'll be out in a minute."

"I have no intention of finishing with you so quick," he tells me as his thumb rubs gentle circles over my throbbing clit.

"What the fuck is taking you so long? The bar is filling up, and I need your help."

"Sorry, I just need a couple of minutes." I bury my face against his neck, inhaling his cologne's spicy, woodsy scent.

"Just get your ass out here," she snaps.

Grabbing Foster's ass, I am on the verge of begging him to pick up his pace. To let me have the orgasm he has so skillfully but slowly been building to explode around him. I hate to admit it, but the thought of being caught is beyond erotic.

"What do you want, Shay?"

"I want—" his thumb circles the other way. My head falls back, and he does not hesitate to kiss my neck.

"You want?"

"I need you to speed up."

"Why?"

"Because I'm so close."

"You want me to make you come?"

"Yes."

"Yes, what?" Apparently, he is as close as I am because he pants his words this time.

"I want to come."

He picks up his pace, driving into me at a frantic tempo. Slamming me against the boxes of stock, they rattle with each thrust. I can't imagine people are oblivious to what is happening in here, but at least the clanging bottles muffle my moans and his growls.

Ten minutes later, I slip out of the stockroom and into the restroom to straighten my clothes. By the time I get back to the bar, Mandy is fuming, Seamus is neck-deep in orders, and Hyde is drinking a beer other than his norm. But I also don't miss Finn's shit-eating grin or the wink Foster gives me. This man is going to be the death of me, I swear to the Goddess.

"What's a girl gotta do to get a drink around here?" A tall, incredibly attractive woman asks. Mandy glares at her but makes no attempt to wait on her. If the eyes of the men in the bar are any indication, they are awe-struck by her beauty. I casually look over toward the one man I hope isn't. Thankfully, he is talking with Atlas and Finn and doesn't seem affected by this newcomer.

"What can I get you?" I ask as I put on the friendliest smile I can manage.

"Whatever," she mumbles as she turns to place her elbows on the bar, allowing her to look around the room. I don't miss the man who grabs her undivided attention. Nor does she hide her fascination as she follows his trek up to the bar.

"Can I get a round?" He asks with his sexy little grin tipping those lips that were between my thighs not twenty minutes ago.

"And just about anything else," she seductively says as she turns to face him. I glance toward the newcomer, an action Foster doesn't seem to miss.

"You can just bring it over to the table when you get a chance," he winks before he turns around. I almost want to give a little fist pump when he doesn't bother to acknowledge her. I'm sure she is not used to being ignored, but I don't give a shit. I hate the jealousy this girl evokes in me, but I don't like sharing, especially where Foster is concerned. My decision to not tell people about us is coming back to haunt yours truly.

"Me—fuckin—ow," she purrs, turning to watch him walk back over to where everyone is sitting. Okay, this chick is pissing me off. Who the hell does she think she is?

"Riona?" Noooo. No way could this be.... "You're early. You weren't supposed to arrive until next week."

Oh no.

"Judging by the caliber of the men around here, I should have come a long damn time ago." She says with a smirk. The entire time never once does she remove her eyes from Foster.

Seamus's niece. Fuck my life.

Episode Seventy-Four: Sonnet

Foster

HEARING SHAY MOAN my name in the stock room is a sound I will never grow tired of, nor the flush of her skin or the heady tone of her voice. I meant what I told her; she is the most beautiful woman I have ever seen, and I would still feel this way if she were not my mate.

When I am not with her, I find my thoughts drifting to her. When Shadow and I go out for a run, the moon is a constant reminder of the wolf she holds, and even the brightest of stars cannot compare to the allure of her eyes.

Are you going to break out in sonnet next? Should I call you Cummings, or do you prefer Shakespeare?

Shut up, furball.

Oh, I know, Keats. Although lame sonnet boy is more accurate.

I said shut up.

What are you gonna do next? Compare her eyes to the brilliance of a million stars, her beauty to the golden hues of dawn's new rays?

You are really starting to piss me off, furball

I'm pretty sure even the chicks up at the bar rolled their eyes at your lame comparison.

You do realize you're the only one who can hear my thoughts. Right, dipshit?

Should I see if I can get your balls back out of her purse, or would you prefer to leave them there? You know, all safe and toasty warm.

Are you done yet?

On the upside, at least they're not blue anymore. Imagine how surprised Shay would be to find a pair of shriveled-up old blue balls next to her ChapStick.

You realize by calling me old, you're calling yourself old, don't you? Sometimes Shadow doesn't think before he speaks.

Maybe she'd mistake them for raisins.... Wait, that's not right, is it?

No, and thanks for realizing.

They're actually closer to a craisin. A sonnet spouting craisin.

Alright, you made your damn point. Now shut the fuck up, furball.

Then stop spouting this bullshit. It's one thing when you tell Shay this shit, but to make me suffer through it —

"Earth to Foster, are you with us?" Ness asks, leaning over and waving her hand in my face, forcing my eyes to focus on hers.

"Yep, just...." Remembering Lindsey is at the table with us, I say, "thinking."

"Well, tune the.... *Thinking,*" she winks at me, indicating she is aware I was talking to Shadow, "out and spend some time with your favorite cousin. Goddess knows we haven't seen you much since we returned from our *trip.*" I can't stop the little chuckle when she wiggles her eyebrows.

After Shay decided she didn't want to make our relationship public yet, I swore Ness to secrecy. And while she has kept the juiciest gossip she has ever been privy to quiet, she takes great pleasure in throwing out these little innuendos.

Before I can go back up to get us another round and flirt with my sexy-as-hell mate—

Is this reference okay, jackass? I ask my smart-ass wolf, Shadow. There are two reasons I do this. I don't want to hear any more bullshit from him tonight, and I hate his new nickname for me.

It's not a sonnet, and she is sexy as hell, so yeah, I'm good with this shit.

Glad I could help.

Hey, I'm just trying to keep your buddies from kicking your ass, dumbass.

—Mandy brings one over for us. And, of course, she has to stay and chat. And by chat, I mean she giggles while finding a reason to touch me seventeen times. Seventeen times in less than the five minutes she stood over here. That's got to be a new record for her. I hope Shay changes her mind about the whole not going public shit soon.

"So, who's the skank?" Ness growls. Whomever she's talking about has definitely roused her ire since she's sitting back in her chair, arms crossed over her chest, bouncing her leg incessantly

"What skank?"

"The redhead who thinks she's all that."

"She is all that and a bag of chips," Finn says, giving Ness a wink.

"You cannot tell me you think she's good-looking."

"I'm not saying that at all."

"Good. I was going to tell you to get your damn eyes examined—"

"What I'm saying is she is fucking sexy as sin," Ness groans, but in all fairness, she should have seen it coming. Finn has always been a huge flirt, and he absolutely has a thing for redheads.

"That's Riona. She's Seamus's niece," Mandy interjects, and if the scowl on her face is anything to go by, I would have to say she is firmly in the not a fan of the new girl boat, sitting right next to Ness.

"Riona, even her name is sexy," Finn rolls the R of the girl's name while wiggling his eyebrows.

"I'll be happy to introduce you to her; maybe she can learn what doesn't belong to her," Mandy snaps. I can assure you her comment does not go unheard by Ness, and there is no way Ness will let it go. In three, two....

"No, Foster sure as shit doesn't belong to her. In fact," My silent glare tells Ness to keep her mouth shut. "let's just say Foster is off the damn table to everyone. Finn too."

"Don't you put Finn in that Foster category," Finch snaps.

"Ah well, that's just grand. Now this chick is onto Atlas. What a skank."

"What?" Finn asks, twisting to see what's happening.

"Nope, strike that she is totally eye-banging you again. I'm gonna beat this chick's ass."

"Eye-banging who?" Finn asks, struggling to keep the girl in his sights in the growing crowd.

"Not you, dipshit," Ness snaps.

"You wound me, Nessie," Finn doesn't see the surly glare Ness gives him since he is on his feet trying to find that chick.

"Ness, do you really think I give a shit? She can stare all day long. It will never happen."

"What will never happen?" Atlas asks, grabbing a chair to join us at our table.

"Oh, the desirable piece of woman leaning against the bar," Finn says with a grin.

"Damn, bro, if you aren't interested, mind if I get her digits?" Denver asks.

"Go for it."

"Hell yeah, you're a good man, Foster. Here goes nothing." Denver smooths his hair before wandering up to the bar, but it must not have gone well since he's back almost as quickly. He tells us she took his drink and promptly started asking about me.

"Is something wrong with Shay?"

"No, quite the contrary; she should be as satisfied as a kitten after a bowl of milk, huh Foss." Finn may be laughing; I'm not.

"Why?" I ask Denver

"I heard her bitching under her breath about ripping out someone's eyes and dunking them in her next drink."

Looking up at Shay, I discover her staring at the new girl. I can't say seeing my sexy mate jealous doesn't give me a little pleasure. Only because I know she feels as strongly about me as I do about her, but she has nothing to worry about. Walking up to the bar, I'm careful to steer clear of Seamus's niece, but it doesn't do me any good because she saunters over to where I'm standing almost immediately.

"Hi."

"Hello," I say to be polite without looking at her, hoping she'll get the message without me having to flat-out turn her down.

"What can I get for you, Foss?" Shay's tone is anything but friendly.

"Surprise me," I tell her with a wink.

"Surprise you?"

"Yep, I discovered earlier tonight that surprises can lead to great things."

"Really."

"The best." This causes a smile to tip those luscious lips of hers.

"Put it on my tab, okay, sweetie," Riona says, reaching across me, dragging her breasts across my arms, all so she can grab a coaster.

Shay doesn't miss Riona's advances, but what Shay does next is something I never expected. Before I can turn Riona down, Shay hops up on the bar, swings her legs to my side, and smashes her mouth against mine in a heated, sexy-as-hell kiss. I am vaguely aware of Riona gasping, followed by her high heels stomping away from us, but I could give a shit less right now because my mate is kissing me, making me think about all the fun things I would rather be doing with her. Possibly right here on this fucking bar.

The raucous cheers from Ness and Finn confirm Riona isn't the only one to see our kiss. When she finally pulls away, she gives me a fiery little grin.

"I told you surprises lead to great things, and you can surprise me like that anytime, beautiful," I tell her before pulling her in for another.

Episode Seventy-Five: Lessons

Brady

SINCE MY UNCLE disowned me and dissolved the bond between his pack and mine, things have improved. I don't know if he thought we would crumble without his support or if I would beg him to reestablish our connection. The answer to both is no; we're doing fine without them.

I released my mother; as pissed as I am at her for the shit she did, she is still my mom. This doesn't mean she will return to the high life when I make it clear to our pack with my mother present; she is no longer the Luna. This way, there is no confusion. And just like all the other wolves in this pack, if she plans on staying and wants to eat, she has to earn her keep like everyone else. If she doesn't like it, she can leave. She is also free to go if she doesn't like the new direction I'm taking the pack in. She can get the hell out of my office if she has anything shitty to say about Shay.

Since Nan left with Shay, I required someone to run the kitchen. It felt only fitting to put my mother there since she made Shay's life a living hell. I figured it was high time for her to learn what it felt like to be forced to cook for two hundred hungry wolves three times a day.

On the first day, I walked in on her with her feet kicked up, champagne in hand, while one of the newer she-wolves was giving her a manicure and two other younger members were doing all the cooking.

That night I forbade anyone from entering the kitchen during the hours my mother was preparing our meals. To say my mother was not happy doesn't begin to cover it. If the smoke coming from her ears was real, let's just say the room would have been filled.

The next day, breakfast was prepared on time, with my mom looking like she had just left the spa. When I questioned Colton, he confirmed no other wolves helped because he sent them all out to either run drills or assist in different areas that needed them. As surprising as this may sound, it was pretty damn good. Lunch was even better, and if it wasn't for a call from the owner of the local catering company, I might not have figured out what she was up to as quickly.

"Brady, my driver broke down, so the food will be a little late. I'm really sorry about this"

"Food?"

"Yeah, twenty trays of homemade lasagna, salad, rolls, and twenty-five pies."

"And the name of the person who put in the order?"

"It was your mom, Adela." Son-of-a-bitch, she is going to be difficult.

So that night, I forbade food deliveries unless cleared by Colton or me first. I also made my mother return all the funds since she used pack money to pay for the catered meals, not her own. And yep, you guessed it, she had a standing order for three meals a day with either the catering company or the local diner for the foreseeable future.

The next morning, I had to stifle a laugh when I walked into the kitchen to find her hair sticking up and disheveled, clothes covered in flour and eggs, one heel broke, and makeup running down her face.

She must learn there are consequences for her actions. To be honest, I think she is getting off easy, yet if you ask my mother, she'd tell you I just handed her a death sentence.

"Your mom burned lunch again, Brady," Colton advises.

"Why does that not surprise me?"

"So, have you given any further thought to Erin's offer?"

"She's welcome to switch from my uncle's pack to ours if that's what she wants, but this is where it ends. I'm not looking for a Luna."

"You can't keep pining over Shay, Brady. It's not good for you or the pack," Maggie says, coming into my office, curling up on Colt's lap before she begins kissing him like I'm not sitting here.

"I have other chairs in the room, Maggie."

"Yeah, but none that kiss like this," she grins.

"If my chairs kissed like that, I'd never leave my office," my response causes Colt and Maggie to burst out laughing.

"You wouldn't need a chair if you—"

"No, Maggie. I'm not looking for anything."

A few of the shifters who left after my ceremony returned to depose me as the Alpha. I don't know if they all believed me weak because I did not fight Foster for the pack, but I can assure you I am not. They show up, issue their challenge, meet me in the circle, and fall by my hand. I am not so cold a leader that I do not offer them an out because I do right up until they shift, and I know there will be no reasoning with them.

Even Owen, a man I grew up around, a man I thought of as family, returned with a handful of shifters to challenge me. But unlike the others, he turned tail and ran when I took down three of them in back-to-back challenges. I guess I shouldn't be surprised; why would a man I only considered to be family stand by me when my own uncle didn't.

My cousin Jason is torn between what my uncle demands and what I believe he knows to be true. He knows of the mistreatment of the pack members; hell, he sees it firsthand since his father treats the members of his pack much the same. What I don't know is if the link between our packs will be restored when he is finally granted Alpha of White Fang or if he will uphold his father's wishes and sever all ties.

"Brady, someone is approaching the front gate." The sentinel advises in a rush.

"Do we know who it is?"

"Never seen them before."

"Well, let's go greet our guest." I can't help but think back to the last time someone unknown to this pack showed up. He turned my world upside down, took someone I cared for, someone I had fallen in love with, and left without a fight.

Colt and Maggie pursue me out to the porch just as the car pulls to a stop. Three men I have never seen before, although there is something familiar about the one who seems to be in charge, move to the front of the SUV but do not advance any further.

"My name is Brady, and this is my community." Unsure who these men are, I do not want to mention the term pack in case these men are nothing more than mortals.

"I know who you are," the biggest one says as he casually leans back against the hood of his vehicle.

"Yeah. That's interesting because I don't have the slightest fucking clue who you are. So, care to share?"

"In due time," he replies coolly as he lifts his eyes to meet mine. The glow around the iris confirms this is no mere man; he's a shifter.

Descending the first step, I am just about to inform him he can either answer now or get the fuck off my land when

Natashia's car comes skidding to a halt behind his, and who I see exiting her car has my blood boiling.

"I see you replaced me as Beta with a weaker, pathetic version of myself. No matter, I could never have followed a spineless Alpha like you."

"I am going to enjoy killing you, Travis."

"Yeah, that is not how I see this interaction happening today."

"And how the hell do you see this shit going?"

"I would like to introduce you to my brother Maximus.... And the future Alpha of this pack."

Episode Seventy-Six: To Bad

Riona

I HATE BEING denied. When I decide I want something, I take it. I don't take no for an answer. Men have never been able to deny me, and I am not about to allow that fine-ass Alpha Foster, and thanks to my uncle, I already know he's the Alpha of their local pack, to be the first. I couldn't care less about his wallflower girl toy. Either she will get on board with me being his Luna, or she can get the hell out of my new town.

But make no mistake, I will rule here.

At least until I can convince Foster to take over a bigger pack in a more prominent area, preferably closer to a large city. I like to be wined and dined, and by the time I'm done with Foster, he will want to fulfill my every fucking desire.

When my mother initially told me I was coming to stay with my uncle in America, I was stoked. Hell, anything had to be better than staying in Ireland, where I had already used up all the men worth a shit. This is until she informed me I would be living in some Podunk little town at the ass end of nowhere.

The second I laid eyes on him, I could sense both the bitches behind the bar were jealous. At least the other chick, Mandy, was smart enough to figure out I planned on taking the object of her desire the instant she saw me. The one with her lips smashed on my future mate. Not so much.

"I highly doubt my uncle is paying you to snog this hot piece of ass or creating a spectacle in the middle of his pub, especially when he has thirsty patrons. So how about you hop to it and get me and lover boy over here a drink, Sam?"

The chick pulls back with her eyes narrowed, yet I notice my future mate only has eyes for her. For now, only for now.

"My name is not Sam; it's Shay. I can spell it if you need me to," she snaps. Too bad I don't give a shit.

Lifting my eyebrow, I glance down at my empty glass, indicating it isn't going to fill itself. With a huff, she spins and drops back down to the other side of the bar to make my drink.

"Name's Riona," I say, offering my hand to Foster.

He looks down at my hand before his eyes crawl back up to my face. And it pleases me to no end when they linger a few beats too long on my amply exposed cleavage.

"Not interested. See you after your shift, babe."

"Sounds good," Shay replies, but her eyes never leave mine.

Taking this opportunity to piss her off further and prove to her their relationship is not as solid as she hopes, I push up closer to Foster before whispering, "Sure about that?"

"Riona, get yer arse back here now," Seamus interrupts.

With the low growl from the chick, who doesn't seem to understand how far out of her league she truly is stepping, I move back, but not before I blow him a kiss and wink at her. Turning, I follow my uncle into the kitchen to the sound of bottles slamming against the bar.

Did I want to walk away from him? No. But I can't have my uncle sending me home before I claim what belongs to me. The slew of cursing as I saunter away from where he is still standing, hopefully getting an eye full of my tight ass, has me grinning.

Yes, this will be fun. Breaking their relationship, claiming what she thought belonged to her, rising to Luna, but mostly mounting this fine-ass man behind me. Deliciously fun.

Walking past the other bitch who wants him, I snap, "Close your mouth and keep your fucking eyes off my future mate."

"Riona! Right. Now."

*****

Following my uncle into the kitchen, he stops so abruptly I almost run directly into him. He's really going to have to get used to how things will be around this place from here on out.

"Why? Why must ya come to me bar and start acting the maggot straight away?"

"Uncle Seamus, I'm only staking my claim to what we both know will be mine sooner or later anyway. After seeing my competition, my bet is on sooner."

"Riona, I think Shay and Foster made it clear tonight that they are together."

"Because he didn't know about me."

"Not a titter of wit this one. You do me head in."

"Uncle Seamus—"

"No. You will back off. Shay's a good girl who hasn't had the easiest go in life."

"And Foster is a fine ass man who hasn't had a woman who knew how to handle him."

"Foster doesn't need your shite. Don't make me send your arse back to Ireland 'fore ya even unpacked."

"You worry too much, Unk."

"Bollocks. Riona, I want you to promise me you won't be the 'egit me know you can be."

"Hand to the goddess uncle Seamus no 'egit here. I'm going to get a wee haf'n'. Want one?" Not waiting for his response, I stroll out and let my eyes settle on the object of my desire. One tall, muscled, handsome Alpha named Foster.

After fifteen minutes of me leaning against the bar with my best come-hither eyes, with him ignoring me the entire time, I realize I may need to come at him from another approach.

If he doesn't respond to flirting, then maybe jealousy will work. And here comes a perfectly delicious fucking specimen to accomplish this.

"Hey," I say, leaning over to run my perfectly manicured nail up his arm.

"Not interested."

"Come on now, don't be like that. Can't a girl be friendly? You know, hoping to make a new friend?"

"Is that what you were doing with my buddy? Trying to be friends?" He turns, giving me a full view of him, and he's just as handsome as Foster. If I hadn't already decided who I wanted, I'd make him mine. In fact, I would have been willing to forgo Foster altogether for this sexy-as-hell specimen before me. The only problem is he's not the Alpha, and I will be the Luna of my own pack. One way or another.

"Right now, I'm only worried about being your friend. So tell me, friend, what's your name? Or should I just keep calling you handsome?"

This grabs his attention long enough for him to shake his head before he laughs at me. Fucking laughs. At. Me. Does he not realize who the hell just spoke to him? But his sexy deep voice reaches in, tickling me in places I now want him to touch. He'll do until I get the one I truly wish to have.

"Still not interested. Have a nice evening; enjoy your hunt."

"Oh, I will," I say loud enough that there's no question he heard me.

"Just like Foster, you should give up on Atlas. He doesn't date the girls in this town." I turn to find the jealous one named Mandy standing there, drying her hands on a towel.

"He doesn't date girls like you from this town. I am not like you," I reply, twisting my hair around my finger. "Besides, I don't want to date him; just fuck him."

The wallflower laughs a snarky little laugh, believing she knows what a man wants better than I do. Well, I have one thing to say to her and the idiot drying her hands.

Game on, bitches. Game on.

Episode Seventy-Seven: Jealous

Shay

"I AM NOT jealous." I scoff as I lean against his desk. Hoping to appear nonchalant, I cross my arms over my chest and one ankle over the other. It's a miserable, epic fail since Foster is now chuckling as he leans back in his chair.

"Really, because I'm pretty sure if you could have shifted, you would have ripped her throat out. Poor Seamus would be down one niece and had a shit ton of explaining to do with his sister."

He shifts in the chair, so now I am pinned between his muscular arms and legs. Even though he has remained seated and I'm looming over him, his dominant presence fills the room and has me thinking about those powerful hands roaming over my body.

For the love of the Goddess, I need to learn how to control these damn hormones.

"Shut up," I say, pushing him away from me, trying to put some space between me and those hungry eyes of his.

Foster, who is unwilling to let this go, doesn't move away. No, quite the opposite; he comes to his feet, pressing me further against his desk

"I think it's sexy."

"What?" I mutter as he presses kisses along my neck.

"That you would actually believe there is any other woman in this world I want other than you."

"Not just anyone, a chick who is drop-dead gorgeous."

"Who gives a shit? My mate happens to be the most beautiful woman to ever grace this world."

"She's confident."

"And you aren't?" He slides his hand under my shirt. His fingers skim along the top of my jeans as his lips brush across mine.

"But she's—"

"Babe."

"Yeah."

"Is this really what you want to talk about right now?" He asks as he unbuttons my pants.

"What? Do you want to do this right here? On your desk?"

"I'm not using it for anything else, so pleasing my mate and making her scream my name would be an improvement. Not to mention if I ever decide to have a meeting in here, I can imagine your sexy body laid across it."

"Don't you think that could be a problem?"

"I'm not seeing the issue," he says as he lowers my jeans.

"A huge distraction from your meeting."

"If you ever had to sit through one of them, you would understand why I welcome the distraction. Besides, either it's the memory of me pleasing you on this desk or the fantasy. I prefer the memory."

"Foster—"

"Sweetheart, I plan on hearing you moan my name one way or another, and I plan on doing it while I drape your sexy ass across this desk." He tells me, pulling my shoes off so he can finally rid me of my jeans. He silences any further objections when he kisses his way up my legs.

His tongue sliding along the lace of my thong, the thong he surprisingly left on when he took off my pants, sends waves of pleasure coursing through me. But his hungry eyes, accompanied by his sinful grin, results in the last bits of my reserve slipping away.

It seems neither one of us can get enough. Especially since I damn near attacked him the minute I got off work last night. I hate to admit part of the reason may have had something to do with Seamus's niece. I guess I was feeling insecure, which is an emotion I hate to admit. So last night I took what I needed to prove nothing had changed between us. It is one of the few times he has ever relinquished control.

This morning it seems he plans to retake it. Foster slowly slides the object, keeping him for his goal, down my legs before tucking them in his back pocket.

"I'm going to need those back."

"No."

"No?"

He shakes his head, confirming I had not misheard him. "Every time I see you today, I want to know I hold the only thing I would ever permit against this sweet pussy tucked safely in my back pocket."

"I'll just put on another pair."

"I'm fine with that, but be aware I will strip them from you too, and just so you know, I don't care where we are when I discover them."

"Bullshit, you would never take my clothes off around another man."

"I'll just order them to avert their eyes while I take what I want." My giggled response is all the challenge he needs.

"You doubt me?"

"I know you're the Alpha, and the wolves here will do as you order, but how do you propose to make the humans in Lake submit?"

"I'll tell you what, sweetheart, after I finish with you here, you run off; put on another pair so I can show you how I plan to make them obey. In fact, from here on out, whenever I find you wearing these sexy little things, I will strip them from you."

I don't know if my gasp is from what he just told me or his tongue running along the wet folds, made wetter by his touch. Collapsing against his desk, I bite my lips, hoping to stifle the moan he is working so hard to elicit.

He knows how close I am when my hands instinctually twist his hair, pulling him closer. Unlike any other time, he does not grant me the release I am on the verge of begging for. No, this time, he leaps to his feet, flips me over, and locks my hands over my head as he thrusts deep inside me.

The sudden shift from the warmth of his mouth to him stretching me around him as he wildly drives inside me has me giving into his desire as I moan his name.

Someone knocking on the door has me trying to pull away from him; however, he refuses to release me. Without stopping his pace, he somehow does what I never could; he growls, "Get the fuck away from my door."

The rhythm he keeps along with his refusal to release me is maddening, and when the pleasure he has so expertly built within me explodes, I don't just moan his name; I scream it. Goddess, I hope whoever was out there left, or I may never be able to look them in the face again.

"I think my sexy vixen enjoys knowing someone is listening."

"No," I try to deny what we both already know. As embarrassed as I know I will undoubtedly be when I see whoever is standing on the other side of that door face to face, it is just as erotic knowing Foss can take me anytime, anywhere, and while anyone is listening.

Grasping my arms in one hand, his free hand brushes along the side of my breasts, around to my quivering stomach, straight between my legs to stroke the throbbing he is responsible for as he continues to fuck me from behind. His mouth next to my ear, whispering all the nasty erotic things he wants to do to me, has me squirming with anticipation.

Fulfilling one of them, he pulls out only long enough to flip me on my back and rip my shirt open, exposing my breast to his waiting mouth before he rams back into me. The sensation sends ripples of pain and pleasure coursing through me.

This time, not even the knocking on the door could stop me from screaming as he pushed me over the brink into wave after wave of euphoric bliss.

"You're mine," He pants against the nipple he held between his teeth.

"Always."

My confirmation is the last piece he needs to lose himself within me. When he has spilled every drop, he pulls me up to smash his mouth against mine. The taste of me lingering on his tongue has me begging him to take me again. Pulling away from me, he fixes his pants before he sits in the chair, his eyes tracing every curve and valley of my exposed frame.

"And as happy as it would make me hearing my name moaned from those sweet lips all day, I've kept Atlas and Denver waiting long enough."

"Don't tell me that's them out there." I whip my head in the door's direction as the reality I now have to walk past two men I have only just gotten to know surfaces.

Fuck. My. Life.

Wiggling into my pants causes a lopsided grin to grace his stupid, handsome face.

"You knew who was out there?"

"Yeah."

"And you still...."

"Pleasured the most ravishing woman in the world until she screamed my name twice?"

With my eyes wide and mouth hanging open, I nod.

"Then yes, I suppose I did." He stands up, putting one hand on either side of my hips, caging me in as he looks down at my still-exposed breast. Slowly shifting his eyes to mine, he tells me in that deep, sexy timbre, "And if you continue to sit there like this, I'll do it again."

Huffing, I try to pull my shirt around me, realizing how pointless it is because he destroyed it when he ripped it open. No matter how I pull or twist, I expose one breast or the other, and there is no way I'm walking out of here like this.

Reaching up, he slides the tattered remains down my arms, leaving me completely bare.

"I don't see how that helped in this situation."

My only answer is the grin he gives as he reaches behind his head to pull off the shirt he somehow kept on. Seeing him standing there, shirtless, muscles rippling with each move, I forget all about the men waiting on the other side of the door as I lift my fingers to skim the planes of his chiseled abs.

The gentle kiss he presses against each breast has the first of what I hope is many more moans rushing out of me. Disappointment fills me when he slides his shirt over my head, ensuring our playtime is done.

"Be back here at one o'clock because I plan to continue right here where we left off," to drive home his point, he strokes his thumb over my nipples, already pebbling with excited anticipation.

"Come on in, guys." What in the hell did he say? No way did he invite them in since he still has me pressed against his desk, thumb exploring my breast, lips skimming the sensitive skin on my neck.

"Woah, my mistake. I thought you said come in," Denver says in a rush.

“Shay was just heading out. But she’ll be back soon, so we need to get this shit handled.” He may be talking to Denver, but his eyes never leave mine. Clearing my throat, I stand to begin my walk of shame.

“Shay.”

“Denver. Atlas.”

“Hello, Shay.” Where I could hear the merriment in Denver’s greeting, Atlas does a much better job hiding his. Regardless, I cannot force myself to meet his gaze as my face heats with my overwhelming embarrassment.

“Morning, Shay,” the sing-song quality of Ness’s voice confirms Atlas and Denver weren’t the only ones to hear our exploits.

Episode Seventy-Eight: Goad

Brady

THESE ASSHOLES THINK they can show up and lay claims to my pack. They are sadly mistaken. Travis and Natashia should know better, and this Maximus can fucking kiss my ass.

"If you wish to claim my Alpha title, come take it."

"In due time, the rest of my companions have not yet arrived," Maximus calmly declares as he leans back against the hood of his car.

"You think you can show up in my pack, declare yourself Alpha, and dictate the terms of how this will proceed?"

"Not only can I, but I already have," he explains with a flick of his wrist. Many of the sentinels I had believed agreed with the direction I was taking our pack turned on me, proving how wrong I actually am. But not just me; they seize any of the wolves who would back me.

My eyes scan the area, seeing my pack members detained or assaulted by the shifters they have lived with their entire life. The sight of such a bitter betrayal has Shade struggling to break free of my control. As much as I want to give in and allow him to tear through the assholes who turned on me and this pack, I need to keep a level head. If I want to save the ones loyal to me, which I do, I need to think and not just leap into the fight these assholes are now controlling.

The smirk covering Travis's face confirms not only did he think this is precisely what I would do, but he is also enjoying this. How could he so coldly attack the men we grew up with or the women we protected? Had there been any lingering doubts he was the monster Shay claimed, they completely dissolved, seeing him as he is now.

"What, are you too chickenshit to face me alone, Travis?" I know him well enough to know he will not allow my challenge to go unanswered. The man he claims is his brother may have restraint, but Travis does not.

"I have never been afraid of you. You strut around this place like you earned the title you cling to so desperately, but you never did shit to earn it. Today you will learn this lesson the hard way."

"That may be, but I can assure you it won't be by you because, make no mistake, asshole, I will take you out long before I fall." My prodding has Travis growling as he steps toward me. Maximus halts him with a hand on his chest.

"I know you're not big on restraint or brains," he mumbles the last part, "but you will use a modicum of both today, little brother."

"Fuck you, Max, I can take him," Travis declares through clenched teeth, his hateful glare never leaving mine the entire time.

"On the one hand, I'm sure you would like to believe this. On the other, I'm not so sure you can." Travis whips his head in his brother's direction, pissed that Max could actually doubt him.

"Don't look at me like that, little brother. You need to learn your limits. I believe this man represents one."

"Bullshit," Travis snaps, but I notice he makes no move to push past Max.

"Be thankful your big brother saved your sorry ass, Travis," I say with a mocking laugh. If I want to sway this encounter in my favor, I need to separate Travis from Max and hope this Maximus doesn't care about his dipshit brother.

Travis begins panting wildly. With each ragged breath he sucks in, he loses himself a little more to his wolf. I know Shade can easily take out his wolf, but I prefer this Max not see Shade until I have him in the circle. No point in giving him any information on what Shade is capable of when I have no intel about his wolf.

"Not only could Shade take care of your puny wolf, but Brady could easily take your ass out," Colt must have caught onto what I was doing; his interjecting pushed Travis past the point of his brother's control. His goading sends Travis into a rage, as evident by the low growl rumbling in his chest and the distinct glow of his eyes.

"Little brother, if you do this shit, you better damn well make sure you win," Max snarls as Travis storms past him.

In his typical showboating style, Travis rips his shirt over his head and throws it to the ground at my feet. He flexes his biceps prior to lunging slightly in my direction. Knowing Travis, this was meant to intimidate me; the response he gets is me laughing at him. I have no fear I won't defeat him, but the quicker I do it, the more strength I will retain for fighting his brother.

"Brady, are you sure about this?" Maggie asks. Her apprehension is almost palpable as she nervously picks at her fingernails.

"You know I can take him, Mags." Her eyes dart to mine. I know if I wasn't preparing for this fight, she would give me seven kinds of hell for calling her this. Did I do it on purpose? You bet your ass I did because right now, I don't need her taking herself out of this fight.

As I descend the porch stairs, Sadie comes around the corner, adjusting her clothes. Evidently, she was out for a run, and while ordinarily, Sadie is never far from Natashia, the pinched eyebrows, slightly parted-lips stare she gives Tosh confirms she did not know about this or their plans to take over my pack.

"Tosh? What's going on?"

"You can't be that dumb, Sad." Natashia declares with an eye roll.

"You know I hate it when you call me that, Tosh, and I have no darn idea what the heck is going on," Sadie's meek response further incited Natashia's ire.

"I told you I would be the damn Luna of this pack."

"But I thought you meant you were going to try to win Brady back over, not remove him as our Alpha."

"Something told me Brady wasn't going to see reason."

"Something should have told you Brady has better taste," I snap.

"Tosh, he's our Alpha."

"Not for long," she declares with a smirk.

I'm looking forward to making them eat these words. Entering the circle, I watch as Travis paces back and forth on the other side. Removing my shirt, I lift my hand to beckon him as I declare, "Come and try to claim what you have always wanted."

And with my challenge issued, Travis charges.

Episode Seventy-Nine: Hiding in Plain Sight

Atlas

"DENVER, IF YOU don't get your ass moving, I'm leaving without you," I yell through the clubhouse. I had promised Foster I would check on the whereabouts of the assholes who took Shay. We're traveling to my other chapter to look into their location, but more importantly, I want to get Denver out of Lake for a few days. I got word the Vanguard was getting ready to make another sweep.

When I selected where I would settle while I searched for answers, I thought Lake would be the perfect quiet place to hide among them. Imagine my astonishment at discovering a pack of wolf shifters outside the town.

At first, I kept my distance from them, knowing their heightened senses would immediately pick up I am anything but mortal.

Coming to this realm was never something I wanted to do, but when someone attempted to end our king's life, I had few options.

The one they accused is innocent. I know he is, and no amount of manufactured evidence will sway my opinion on this matter because the man charged is my best friend and someone you know well, Denver.

I believe Ayaan is the man responsible for the attempt on our King. Unfortunately, prior to me bringing him before the court for judgment, he was tipped off, allowing him to slip away. He is hiding somewhere within this realm. Until I find him, I will not rest because I am more than just King Citron's warrior…. I am his firstborn son.

As my father lingers on the edge of life and death, I search for Ayaan and the answer I believe he holds to what ails my father. I do this because my father is a good and honorable king. I do this because he's my father, and I love him, but if I am being truthful, I do this because I have no desire to rule.

My youngest brother Rayden and my father's most trusted council member, Uriah, send updates on his prognosis. He remains comatose, but the most important thing is he remains. Alive yet not. While I have no desire to linger on this plane any longer than necessary, I have not yet found my target.

As shocked as I was to discover the pack, I will not leave because they serve a purpose. This simple objective is to conceal my friend from the Vanguard hunting him. And even if only two of the wolf shifters know about us, they do everything they can to keep Denver safe. I can't explain how they mask us. The only thing I can come up with to describe it is that having so many supernatural beings in such a confined area must screw with their abilities.

The longer we remain here, the closer I have grown to them. Foster and Finch were not what I expected, but they earned my respect when they could have disclosed where we were during one of the vanguard's sweeps, but instead of winning favor with them, they hid us. Taking a chance, I revealed who I truly am, and they showed me who they were.

Since then, they have become like brothers to us. This, in part, is why I help them and will continue to do so until we settle Foster in as their new pack leader. I think his mate Shay is good for him. He seems calmer when he is around her, less burdened since Foss finally admitted how he felt about her. It took him long enough to realize it.

"Hey Atlas, you ready to ride?" I made the mistake of introducing Denver to the world of motorcycles; since then, he can't get enough. The dumbass wants us to ride to Denver in near-freezing temperatures. Here's the thing, like most non-mortal beings, the elements don't affect us, yet trying to explain how we rode for two hours in these temperatures to the mortal world is not so easy.

"Are you sure you don't want to take the truck?"

"Is that even a question?"

"I posed it in the form of a question, so technically, yes."

"Hard pass. Can't feel the wind in my hair inside your truck."

"Explain to me how you feel the wind in your hair since you pull the shit up in your girly bun."

"It's called a man-bun, and the honeys love it."

"Ah-huh. Let Madge hear you calling women honeys, and you won't have working man parts left to worry about them."

"Madgie loves me, don't you, Madge?"

"Depends. What stupid shit did you say or do now?" Madge is the woman I hired to run the bar at my club. I didn't plan on starting an MC, but it morphed into one over the last year we have been here. They are another source of concealment since the Vanguard is looking for two men traveling alone.

"Calling women of the world honeys," Freddie yells. Freddie is one of our newest members. Oh, and his name isn't truly Freddie; it's Blake, but the guys took to calling him Freddie on account of him looking like some actor from the nineties.

Madge doesn't have to reply. She has one of those looks that can keep even the toughest of us in line, and right now, she has it firmly settled on Denver, who is suddenly looking very sheepish. The booming laughter from the guys at the bar has Denver rolling his eyes.

Deciding to give my buddy a break, I clap my hand down on his shoulder and tell him, "Get your man-bun-wearing ass on the bike. We need to hit the road before it gets any later."

"Can I expect you boys back tonight?" Every time she calls us boys, I want to laugh. To this world, Denver and I look like we're in our twenties, but in reality, we're several hundred years older than that.

"Probably not. I'm looking into something for my buddy, so we'll probably crash at the apartment there in Denver."

"You two, be careful."

"Will do. Call if you need anything," I tell Madge before giving her a quick peck on the cheek.

*****

By the time we pull into the parking lot of our Denver chapter, the party is already in full swing, but thankfully Mick is still sober enough to update us on what they found.

"They're heading north."

"Isn't Shay from up north somewhere?" Denver asks.

"Yeah. Any idea where they were heading?"

"Nah, my contacts just said North."

"What about the other thing?"

"No word on that front yet, brother, but we're on it."

"Damn, it's like Ayaan just fell off the planet," Denver grumbles after Mick walks away.

"Don't worry, he'll show up somewhere, and when he does, we'll nab him." Here's hoping we find him before my father dies and Denver goes down for it.

Episode Eighty: Uninvited

Foster

"YOU'RE SURE."

"According to my contacts, yeah." Frustrated, I drop my eyes and immediately see the faint imprint of her perfect ass on my desk. Flashes of her laying under me moaning short-circuits any other thoughts.

"So, how is Shay getting along?" Atlas apparently sees where my eyes have settled. After the show we put on, they have to know the desk had a starring role, and this alone has him asking his question with a semblance of couth.

Denver, not so much. "After what we heard coming from the room, I would say she was pretty fucking satisfied."

"Shut up," I say with no real malice in my response as Atlas smacks the back of his head.

They fill me in on the rest of their trip, telling me anything they feel will assist me with finding the asshole who took Shay.

Shadow and I have some unfinished business with that fucker and his brother.

Damn straight, we do. Shadow growls.

After talking to Atlas, I did something I never thought I would. I tried to reach out to my father's other son. You know, the only one who mattered. I wanted to warn him he may have trouble heading his way. Unfortunately, his phone keeps going straight to voicemail.

I've kept tabs on him since I left, and it seems he's doing precisely what he promised Shay; making changes. All the changes he's made seem to be for the betterment of his pack and the wolves who remain. Lending credence to his statements and, in the process, has me liking him if only a little bit.

Electing to make one last attempt, I call the number Shay gave me for their pack house. But like Brady's cell, this phone just rings endlessly. It's unusual for the pack phone to go unanswered, but not alarming, so I'll try again later. Right now, I have a much more pressing issue to deal with. The one person in this world I never thought I would find standing at my office door happens to be the exact person I discover there. Riona.

Fuck, Shay is going to lose her shit if she finds this girl and me alone in my office.

"How did you get in here?" Someone from the pack should have seen this girl wandering on pack land and stopped her to ask what she was doing. At the very least, someone should have escorted her until they knew she wasn't a danger to the pack.

"With my two very long, extremely flexible legs," her response is meant to be sexy, and if there was any question about what her innuendo means, the way she is sliding her hands up her legs lays any doubts to rest.

"Okay, so why are you standing at my office door?"

"I came to position for a spot." Does this girl know about us? I always knew Seamus had family that was part of the shifter community even though he isn't, I never asked for details, and he certainly didn't offer them.

Making my response a cautious one, "A spot?"

"Within the pack."

"Pack?"

"You're cute when you get all protective of your pack, but I suppose that's what a good Alpha is supposed to do. Right, Foss?"

"My friends call me Foss; I don't know you."

"But you do know my uncle Seamus. Who, if I'm not mistaken, has helped this pack on more than one occasion."

"Seamus has helped his friends."

She strolls into my office, pausing only long enough to close the door. "Don't do that."

"Do what? The only thing I'm doing is positioning for a place with your pack."

Before I can say anything, she rips her shirt over her head. Normally, this is not abnormal within a wolf pack, nor would it be an issue if she were a member, but Riona is not a member. Besides, she's not wearing a bra, and the bigger problem is Shay really dislikes this girl.

When I see her hands drop to her pants, I yell, "Stop!"

"Are you shy, Alpha?"

"No. I simply don't allow random women to appear in my office and begin stripping."

"Afraid you might like what you see." She runs her hand over her exposed nipple.

"Absolutely no worries there. I am concerned about having to clean blood out of my carpet if Shay walks in here and finds you like this."

"I think I can handle the mousy girl from the bar."

Shadow growls when she says this. While her comment pissed me off, I am more frustrated that she is still standing here with her tits on display and pants undone. Seeing she obviously is not going to redress herself, I walk around my desk, grab her shirt off the ground and toss it back at her.

"First, I wouldn't be so sure about that. Second, don't ever show up in my office uninvited again, and third—"

"What the fuck is going on here?" Shay growls. Fuck, I knew this shit was going to happen.

"Why the hell are you standing here with no shirt on?"

Shit of all times for Shay and Ness to show up here; now wasn't the time. How in the hell am I ever going to be able to convince Shay nothing happened with this girl standing here half fucking dressed. Hell, if I had walked into this situation, I would have already torn the other man apart.

Shay is beyond pissed. She's fucking furious, and her eyes remain glued to the object of said irritation, Riona. I might have missed the subtle shift to signal Moon pushing to take control if I hadn't committed to memory every detail of her beautiful eyes.

"I'm merely trying to prove to my new Alpha the value my wolf can offer."

"Put your freaking shirt back on, you damn cow," Ness hisses. While Shay's full attention is on Riona, mine is on her. So when she clenches her fist repeatedly and her breathing increases, I know she is losing control.

Moving in front of Shay, I tilt her chin up until I have her attention. "Nothing happened in here. I promise you."

Shay takes several deep breaths. Thankfully, the glow in her crystal eyes begins slowly fading.

"I don't know what everyone is so jazzed up about. We do this all the time at our packs back home."

Why does this chick not understand the value of keeping her mouth shut?

Without taking her eyes off me, Shay snaps, "This is not your home, and it sure as shit is not your pack—"

"It is now." Riona's snarky response has a deep growl coming from the other two women standing in the room with us.

"I don't give two fucks if your pack at home has orgies on the regular don't ever fucking do this shit again," Shay slams her mouth against mine before she turns and storms away.

"Where are you going?" I ask as I step out into the hall. This also gives my unwanted guest a chance to get her shit on and vacate my office. I hope Riona takes the hint before Ness tosses her ass out the window.

"To have a fucking conversation with my boss."

Episode Eighty-One: May The Best Man Win

Brady

TURNING AWAY FROM his incoming attack, Travis stumbles, and before he can regain his footing, I am across the ring again. I have no fear of facing Travis. Hell, after what I found out he did to Shay, I am looking forward to it. Not just the beating part, the part where I humiliate him, where I remind him he's nothing and has no control over his own body. Today I make him regret ever touching her.

"Ya know what, big brother, I just might claim Alpha for myself after I beat this puny fucker to death."

"You go on and keep telling yourself that shit, dumbass," Maximus calmly declares as he leisurely leans back against the car with his arms crossed over his chest.

It's amazing how these two dipshits keep talking about taking my position like I'm already defeated. I'll deal with Maximus in a second; right now, Travis is my only focus. Travis spits on the ground at my feet as we circle each other.

"Oh, how the mighty has fallen," Travis laughs.

"If you're talking about the low-life in front of me, then yeah, I guess he has."

"Low-life? At least this low-life didn't ride on my daddy's shirttails. Pathetic."

"That's fucking rich; a piece of shit rapist, calling me pathetic." Maximus's booming laughter makes me wonder what the hell is with this guy.

"He's got your number, little brother."

"I didn't rape anyone."

"Not for lack of trying," Max confesses as he slices a piece of apple.

"Shut up, Max. I don't have to rape anyone. The bitches all line up to ride my fuckin' cock." His brother responds by lifting one finger before curling it down. "What the hell is that supposed to mean?"

"I think he's calling you a limp dick." Max's chuckle confirms to his brother what the rest of us have already figured out.

"Whose fucking side are you on?" When his brother's only response is a grin, I take a chance to push the issue.

"It seems not yours," I laugh, resulting in a growl from Travis.

Travis swings, and it misses my face by only inches, but my return jab catches him off guard. The whoosh of air he expels as he stumbles away from me prevents me from landing the second shot. Faster than I would like, he recovers and lunges at me again. I have no illusions that my one hit would end this fight so easily, but it would have been nice.

When he swings, his fist connects with my jaw; unfortunately, I'm not fast enough this time, sending me stumbling back. Unlike me, he doesn't hesitate to follow as he continues his assault. He grabs the back of my shirt and pulls me down as he brings his knee up. The impact knocks the wind out of me. Knowing he won't stop, I scamper to put some distance between him and me.

He dives, taking my feet out from under me. Twisting at the last second, I land on top of him, giving me the upper hand. I will not squander this opportunity to end this fight quick. Slamming my head down, I hit my mark, and the crunch of his nose as it breaks is a satisfying sound.

His eyes shift as his wolf tries to take over, but having grown up with Travis, I know he wants nothing more than to prove he can defeat me without using his wolf. A memory from our childhood floods my thoughts.

"I can still beat you," Travis pants.

"Your only hope is if you somehow gain your wolf early, butthead." I laugh as I push my weight against his arms harder.

"I promise you, I will beat you one day, and I'll do it without my wolf. Then I'll be Alpha."

"You can't be the Alpha unless you can beat the Alpha, dumb-dumb."

"Yeah, that's what I said."

At eight years of age, Travis was a skinny, weaker version of the man standing before me. I always believed it was all said in jest, but seeing him now fighting to hold his wolf at bay as he lands another blow, I knew he meant every word of his declaration all those years ago.

How could I have been so blind not to see him for what he truly is, an asshole who has always been jealous of me and my position within the pack?

"Brady." My mom's shout is the distraction Travis needs to sway this battle in his direction. Before I can react, he has me on my back, delivering one blow after another, and unlike when we were kids, Travis outweighs me by twenty pounds of sheer muscle.

Looking around the man currently beating me, I can barely see Colt struggling to break free from Owen, my father's old beta, as my mom is being led over to Maximus. Rage replaces all other emotions as an adrenaline surge floods my bloodstream, granting me the extra strength I need to buck Travis off me.

Travis may be bigger than me, but he is not faster. Before he can right himself, I am back on top of him; this time, it is my turn to beat him repeatedly, and I don't hold anything back.

Travis switches from trying to overpower me to hoping to protect himself from my constant assault. I am preparing to deliver the killing blow when my head snaps to the side as my body flies off of Travis. Shaking my head to clear the confusion, I look up to find Maximus standing over Travis.

"I told you, little brother, if you were going to fight him, you better damn well make sure you win."

What I figured was about to happen doesn't as Max yanks Travis to his feet. As the adrenaline surge dissipates, I find it more difficult to regain my footing, but I don't miss Colt breaking through the crowd as he bolts toward Maximus.

Just as Colt arrives, Max sidesteps and snakes his arm around Colt's neck. Seeing my beta and best friend in trouble, I stumble to my feet as I yell, "What it takes two of you to fuckin beat me?"

"My brother was stupid; I'm not."

"Let my Beta and my mother go."

"Or what?"

"Or I'll kill you."

"I'm sure you believe that, but there is one thing you should know about me."

"Yeah, what's that, asshole?"

"I don't fight fair." Before I can move, Max plunges a knife into Colt's side before ripping it out and shoving it into his stomach.

"No!" The roar comes from Shade as much as it does from me as I rush in their direction. Just before I arrive at the spot Max has tossed my lifeless friend, Travis grabs me from behind. Everything from here moves in slow motion. I hear Maggie's desperate screams, and I see most of my sentinels taken out by the ones who accompanied Max. I see my uncle holding my mom as she screams they promised not to hurt me. But it's the look of triumph covering Max's face as a sharp pain pierces my chest I am most confused about.

That is, until my world goes dark.

Episode Eighty-Two: Show and Tell Time

Shay

"SEAMUS, WHY DIDN'T you tell me your damn niece is-is...."

"A whore." Ness finishes for me. Okay, so maybe I wasn't going to go with such a crass statement, but what's done is done, and we cannot take it back. Even though I know she is trying to help me, I give Ness a side-eyed glance to let her know it is unnecessary.

"Bollocks, what 'as she gone and done now?"

"Oh, just stripped in Foster's office," Ness gripes.

"Actually, it's everything," I say as I move my glare from Ness over to Seamus. "Riona came in here all but declaring herself queen of the damn place. Spouting shit about being the next...." Realizing I almost said Luna, I stop myself just before the word tumbles past my lips since I am unsure what Seamus knows about us and what he doesn't.

"Girl always did fancy herself a damn Luna."

Okay, so he knows more than I realize. And I say I because Ness doesn't seem surprised by him saying this. With me not being a part of the pack, I do not know who is a shifter and who isn't, but I have never seen him out on pack land. Which can mean one of several things. Either he isn't a part of the pack, he doesn't regularly take part in the pack's business, or he is not a shifter at all. I have never gotten the sense he could have a wolf, nor has he ever given me any sign he was. So I am leaning toward the whole *"he's not a shifter"* thing, but I've been wrong about stuff like this in the past. Regardless of what he is or isn't, it's high time he explains his affiliation with the pack and why his niece is actin the egit'... igot'... oh fuck it, asshole.

So my Irish slang still needs some work.

"Luna?"

"Aye, this is what me said."

"What do you know about being a Luna?"

"Tichy, are ya slagging me?"

"Not sure what slagging means." He mumbles several things more to himself than to Ness and me. I look over at Ness to see if she understands what he is saying, but when she shrugs her shoulders, I know she doesn't understand him any better than I do.

After several seconds he stops his tirade, leans his beefy frame against the sink, and works to bring his breathing under control. His face is almost as red as his hair.

"Does me head in. Bollocks. Okay, Tichy, come on."

"Where are we going?"

"If we're gonna do this, I need a wee half'n'. Hell, maybe two," Seamus says as he strides through the swinging door to get the drink he believes we both need. Walking out to the bar, I sit on the opposite side as Seamus grabs three glasses and a bottle of the good stuff. A fine scotch only a few people drink. Thankfully, one of those people happens to be the man who's pouring.

Over the next hour, Seamus tells me everything. He confesses while he himself did not inherit the gene necessary to shift, the rest of his family did. His sister despised he was 'normal' while she had to exist in a world not yet ready to come to terms with all things abnormal. And this is how she viewed herself, abnormal. Where he always longed to be like the rest of his family.

Seamus considered himself to be the unlucky one but was always thankful the pack his parents belonged to didn't eject him. Moreover, when their Salutary took him under his wing to teach him all things healing, Seamus found his calling... one he believed would continue until his last breath. Apparently, his last breath happened when a rogue shifter attacked the love of his life and left her for dead. By the time they found her, there was nothing they could do.

His confession about losing her broke my heart, but when he told us she was pregnant with his child, I could not stop the first tears from spilling over. Even as I tried desperately to wipe them away, the surge of emotions he feels glistens brightly in his green eyes as he looks past me to remember the woman and child the wolf deprived him of.

It took him two years, five months, three hours, and forty-six seconds, yes he remembered it right down to the second, to find the shifter responsible for their death and thirty-two seconds to end him. He didn't shoot the shifter; he killed him with his bare hands, wanting to look into the eyes of the man as his life slipped away. He wanted to know that the one who made her suffer was just as scared as she most likely had been.

After returning to his pack, he was never the same, and as much as he wanted to remain one of their healers, he no longer had the heart. He stayed with the pack for the sake of his parents and sister, who was newly married and heavy with a pup.

His dad died next from some rare disease only a handful of shifters acquire, and his mom followed shortly after. His sister lost her mate when another pack attacked theirs. Seamus continued to stay because he felt obligated to help her raise the child. Figuring if he couldn't have one of his own, he could put all the love filling his heart into her baby.

He did this until his sister met a new man, fell in love, and married for a second time. Shortly after their wedding, her new husband asked them for their permission to adopt Narissa. Seamus confessed he was a good man and treated his sister and niece like the sun rose and set only for them, so he was happy to give his new brother-in-law his consent. A year later, Riona joined their family.

This was when he decided it was time to make a new life for himself. He traveled from Ireland to the states and settled in a small community on the Eastern seaboard. He made several trips back to Ireland every year to visit with his sister, but mostly to see his nieces.

And just as his brother-in-law doted on Narissa, he did the same for Riona. Unlike Narissa, Riona took advantage of his kind heart. From the very beginning, she took all the love her dad heaped on her and Narissa and used it against him. Where Narissa was sweet, caring, and a wonderful young lady. Riona was demanding, abrasive, and overbearing.

He tried to tell his sister she needed to gain control of his young niece, but nothing she could do had any positive effect on Riona. Even Narissa moved across Ireland to escape her sister and the games she played.

Seamus's trips grew further and further apart, and when he moved from the eastern seaboard to Lake, they stopped altogether. He had hoped that when his brother-in-law passed away, Riona would stop her shit, but it only got worse until they forced his sister out of the pack when Riona tried to seduce the Alpha.

Her behavior has only escalated since then, and as much as he wishes she would not have come to stay with him, he couldn't turn his back on his sister when she needed him.

He then told me how he met and ultimately confessed everything to Foss and Finn when they found him on their pack land gathering flowers. Not any ordinary flowers but ones the shifter community used for healing. They knew he had to understand what the flower represented because it only works on shifters. The mortal world would have no knowledge of their healing properties, which meant one thing: he was more than just a mere man.

It seems Foster and Finch were none too happy at first and only relaxed after he could answer each and every question they asked him. He told them he was gathering the flowers to send back home to his sister because she no longer had access to their salutary after his niece's stupid actions forced them out of their pack.

Since that day, he has kept their secret, and they watched over him.

He also told me he was the one who removed my collar. Something I will never be able to thank him enough for.

With my head swirling from everything he confessed as much as from the alcohol, I shuffled toward the exit, but his last confession was the one thing I needed to hear more than anything else.

"Riona may be actin' the maggot, but don't you worry yer head bout her."

"Why?"

"Cause I've been around that boy since he was a wee one, and I've never seen Foster happier since he found you, Tichy."

Episode Eighty-Three: Clocks Ticking

Atlas

THERE ARE ONLY a few places I don't feel like I have to be on continual guard. These places include Stooges, Foster's cottage, and the clubhouse Denver and I created. Everywhere else, I worry the Vanguard may show up at any time to pull my best friend back to our realm.

I fear my time for finding Ayaan is running out. Because when my father dies, I will have no choice but to return to claim his seat. Not because I want it but because the realm and court expect it of me. Other family members could do it; I'm not willing to risk the changes they will undoubtedly make regarding the kingdom my father has ruled over.

His subjects.... No, my father always hated this word because he felt he owed his allegiance to the people who followed him. He didn't care if they were among the elite or the lowliest peasant. He felt every man and woman who called him king was worthy of his respect. A trait he passed on to me and something I will uphold regardless of what may happen.

The souls living within my father's realm are special; many represent the last of their line. So it will be my job when my father is no longer in our world to protect them as he has.

I was so lost in thought that I missed one of the club members coming in with someone who shouldn't be here. Imagine my surprise when she saunters up and presses her body between me and the stool next to us.

Groaning, I try to ignore her as I let the heat of the perfectly aged bourbon slide down my throat. But the longer she stands here with her body pressed against mine, the more irritated I get she's in my place to begin with.

"What are you doing in my club?"

"Currently waiting for the bitch—" the glare I flash in her direction confirms it would be prudent if she did not continue this thought. Madge is like family, and I will not have some half-wit chick disrespecting her here. "Perfectly lovely—"

"Better," I snap as I turn my attention back to my drink and the mirror behind the bar.

"Glad to know I could please you."

"Let's get one thing straight, okay. You can't do shit for me. Now, why don't you tell me how you got into my private club?"

"I was invited."

"By whom?" Turning, she waves at one of the younger members. An asshole I regret having let join the club since he has turned out to be a hothead who refuses to obey my simple rules. All rules that I put in place to protect my best friend. One of the more important rules is don't bring people into my club without me vetting them first.

"Of fuckin course, it was Blaze."

"Oh, are you jealous?" She asks, trailing her finger up my arm.

Glancing at her from the corner of my eye, I snap, "No worries there, sweetheart."

"Sweetheart. We're making progress."

Spinning to face her fully, I growl, "What are you doing here? I thought you would be out chasing after another man who doesn't want anything to do with you."

"Don't worry, Foster will claim me as his mate soon enough, but until then, a girl has needs. Desires I've decided you will fulfill perfectly. I like large men, and if I had to guess, I would say the size of these hands is only rivaled by the size of your cock." she purrs as she slides her hand up the inside of my thigh. Pushing her hand away, I've had about as much as I will take from this shifter.

"I already told you once I'm not interested."

"I already told you once you may not be interested yet... but you will soon. I must admit I get wet just imagining you between my thighs. Tongue chasing, eyes wide—"

"Never going to happen. I don't entertain little girls who chase after my buddies."

"And I promise you it will happen. One way or another, I always get what I want, and what I want right now is you," Riona tells me before leaning close enough to run her tongue along my neck.

"Blaze, come get your…." I almost call her something my father would have my head for, so after pausing, I finish with, "date."

I grab the bottle Madge left in front of me and stand before informing her, "Madge, I'll be in my office if you need me."

"No problem," Madge replies as she eyes Riona suspiciously.

I don't miss the smirk Riona has covering her face, nor am I stupid enough to think she won't try to follow me, so to make it clear she is not welcome here, I announce, "Alone, and I do not want to be disturbed. Give this young lady one drink, and then she's leaving."

"Hey man, she's with me," Blaze interjects.

"Then I guess that means you'll also be leaving after one." I don't wait for his response as I ascend the stairs to my office. I know Madge well enough to recognize she won't let little Ms. Flirt anywhere near the stairs now, and by the time I finish my call with Mick, Madge will have bounced her ass out of here.

*****

Riona

Mm-mmm, but I do love a challenge. And next to Foster, this Atlas guy is quickly becoming one of my favorites. I can't wait until I finally bend him to my will. I know I will thoroughly enjoy watching him on his knees, pleasing me.

He may be running now, but not for long.

He could have made things a little easier on me by not attracting the attention of the idiot who brought me here. Or by all but declaring his office off-limits. Especially since this old bitch behind the bar refuses to take her eyes off me now.

Then again, he just made the hunt that much more delicious, and even though he does not know who or what I am, these idiotic mortals should learn one simple rule... fucking with a wolf could be hazardous to your health.

"Hey babe, what are you doing?" the idiot who believes he has any chance with me asks as he drapes his arm around my shoulder. He doesn't have a hope in hell of claiming me unless I can't figure out how to get upstairs; then, I may need this dumbass to fulfill my needs. He's sadly mistaken if he thinks I will be the one on my knees doing the pleasing.

"Currently waiting on my drink." The bitch behind the bar glares at us before shifting her eyes toward the staircase.

"One, and then you're out of here."

"We may have a couple."

Blaze's barked response doesn't seem to affect the old battleax as she growls back, "One."

"I don't take orders from you." Blaze snarls.

"And I don't take them from you," she comes right back as she pours me a single shot.

"It's okay, handsome. Atlas never said how fast I had to drink it," I declare with a wicked grin as I take the tiniest sip possible. Blaze laughs, but the old bitch takes offense and does the one thing she shouldn't, which is taking something that belongs to me.

She tries to make her point when she rips the shot out of my hand, gulping it down before she says, "Oh, would you look at that? It appears you're all done. Time to fucking go."

As I am preparing to snatch out and slam her face against the bar, like a good obedient dog, Blaze does it for me when he grabs this old bitch by her hair, snarling, "Get her another."

"Fuck off, Blaze."

"Who the hell do you fuckin think you are, you old bitch? You need to learn your place." As good as he has been at handling the old bitch while trying to prove himself to me, it all falls to shit when another growl echoes around the room.

"Who the hell do you think you are putting your fucking hands on her?" Denver. Damn, not who I was hoping for. This big dumb ox will only fuck things up further.

Grabbing Blaze by the hand, I whisper in the sexiest voice I can manage, "Come on, baby, why don't you show me how good you are at handling that hog of yours."

Of course, he does exactly what I knew he would, which is to believe I mean his dick when I was actually talking about his bike. I'll let this asshole service me since it doesn't appear I'll be getting Atlas on his knees tonight; this idiot will have to do. C'est la vie.

Episode Eighty-Four: Training

Shay

"HEY FINN, HAVE you seen Foster lately?" I ask, walking into Foster's office.

"Nope, he went out for a run, and then he was going to work out with our sentinels. Did you need something other than my cousin's sweet lovin?"

"Oh... You're hilarious, Finn," I say with a laugh as I leave him relaxing in Foster's office. Finch may be a jokester, but when push comes to shove, I know he will protect Foss with his last breath. This, in part, is why I adore the guy so much, right down to his corny jokes.

"Did you find Foss yet?" Ness asks as she runs up next to me when I exit the packhouse.

"No, he's working out. So I'm just heading over now."

"Ahh, so you wanna watch my cousin get all hot and sweaty for a different reason?"

"What is it with you and Finn? Is sex the only thing you two ever think about?"

"Why the hell not? It is so deliciously fun," she giggles as we begin our trek to the training quarters.

While not quite as impressive as the quarters from Brady's pack, the training area here is still nicer than most gyms used by normal people. It has a room filled with weight equipment, treadmills, and elliptical machines. Hell, it may be easier to tell you what it doesn't have. They devoted another room to master climbing. With the mountains surrounding this area, they must be adept climbers to traverse the terrain as easily as they do. There is a sparring ring filling one room inside and a mock fighting ring outside

"I think it's about time for you to try the climb," Ness declares as I stand at the bottom of the mammoth rock wall looking up at the wolves who are making quick work ascending it.

"Yeah, someday."

"No time like the present," she says as she jingles a harness in front of me. Looking up, the kids are the only pack members wearing harnesses. There is no way I want to make a fool of myself in front of the entire pack. Half of the she-wolves around here already treat me like a social leper, but in all fairness, the other half is very accepting. No point adding fodder for the cannon for the ones who don't trust me yet.

"Hard pass."

"Come on, goofball," Ness laughs as she tosses the harness to the shifter helping the kids. As we move through the complex, I question if Foster ever came here or if we missed him. Until we hear the roars coming from the outside ring.

I find who I've been looking for as we exit the building. Foster is standing in the middle of the training circle fending off wave after wave of newly shifted wolves. At first, my heart leaps into my chest as memories of him in the ring fighting Tobias surge to the forefront, but when I see him laughing, I take my first real breath since walking out here.

Each wolf who attempts to take him down leaves the ring to back slaps and "maybe next time" while Foster fends off the next one charging. The sun glistens across the sheen of sweat covering his muscled frame, and it doesn't take me long to become lost in the ripple of his muscles as he moves.

Watching him fight is as much a turn-on for me as it is training for the young wolves surrounding him. After the last wolf limps out of the ring, Foster turns in a slow circle asking, "No one else? Don't tell me you're all giving up that easily. Come on, there has to be someone who can give me a run for my money."

In a momentary lapse of judgment, I let a not-so-clever idea take form. And like the idiot I am, I do something I never thought I could; I step across the rope marking the edge of the fighting ring as I quietly declare, "I will."

Foster turns to face me, a sexy wicked grin tipping those perfect lips I would rather be kissing. Get your head into the game, Shay; you told him you'd fight him, not fuck him. But this doesn't stop the delicious waves of heat pooling low in my core.

"She might be the only one who can bring you to your knees, cuz," Finch yells over the hushed crowd.

"That she can," he says as he stalks toward me. Not willing to give in to the pounding need pulsing through me, I circle left, forcing him to follow my trek.

"Get him, Shay," Ness yells.

"I got fifty on Foster," one wolf I have only spoken to a hand full of times yells as he flashes the cash.

"I'll take that action," Finn replies, holding up his bet. "Don't let me down, Shayster."

Foster dips to take out my legs, But I sidestep at the last second, barely avoiding him. As I pass, I tap him on the back of his head to prove he was not fast enough.

"That's a girl. Keep it up," someone from the crowd yells as several others cheer my success. Placing my hands together, I lift them and give a celebratory fist wave as I listen to Foster laughing behind me.

Quicker than I can react, Foster scoops me up and throws me over his shoulder as he smacks my ass. Squirming, I dislodge myself enough, so he has to put me down or risk dropping me.

"You're lucky, beautiful."

"Maybe this was my plan all along," I reply with some extra sass.

"I wasn't talking about me capturing you."

"What, pray tell, were you referring to then, oh magnanimous Alpha?" I ask as I sidestep his snaking arm.

Once again, he rushes forward, grabbing me from behind. He pulls me tight against him as his lips brush my ear so he can quietly elaborate, "You're lucky you aren't wearing any of those sexy little panties."

My face flushes as heat races to my cheeks, remembering his promise to rid me of them anytime he caught me wearing them, no matter where we were when he discovered them. His hand snakes down, patting my hip right where the panties would have been. Had I been wearing any, that is.

Before I can stop him, he scoops me up and lies me on the ground while using his body to pin me in place. An auditable sigh surrounds us, and quite a few cheers as they believe I am defeated. Using my long legs, I wait for him to do what I know he will, running his fingers over my cheek. The second he does, I shift, throwing my weight and using my legs; I end up straddling him with his arms pinned against the ground.

"I win."

"Actually, having you straddling me like you are, I'm pretty sure I'm still winning." He lifts his hips just enough for me to feel his growing erection as heat floods all the parts he is currently grinding against. If we were alone, I would be extremely happy to explore this further, but we're not, so I jump up to declare my victory before I say fuck it and continue what he seems only too happy to start.

"She got you, Foss," Finch laughs as he charges me, throwing me on top of his shoulders to give me a victory lap.

"She most certainly does," Foster says, pulling me from his cousin's shoulders. Cheers fill the air when he dips me back, kissing me in front of the entire pack.

As much as he wanted to continue what we had started, he had a few things to finish up, and I wanted to grab some clean clothes from my place, so we agreed to meet up at his cottage in two hours.

Rushing around my house, I have almost everything ready to head out to Foster's place when someone knocks on my front door. Figuring it's Ness here to give me a ride, I run to the door, but who I find standing there takes me by surprise.

Maggie. She's so pale I worry she is going to faint. Her pleading eyes are puffy and red from crying, but the most startling part is the dry blood she is covered in.

"Shay, we need your help. Please."

Episode Eighty-Five: Clinging to Life

Shay

MAGGIE CHOKED OUT as much as she could between her sobs. She tells me all about Travis and Max showing up to challenge Brady. This didn't surprise me, but when Maggie confessed that Natashia and Sebastian were involved, I realized how epically fucked Brady was without even knowing. I almost choked to death when she told me Adela knew and condoned what they had planned.

"We need to get them help," I spin to find someone I never thought I would have to see again standing at my door. I advance as I let a menacing growl escape me, but Maggie jumps between us.

"What the fuck is she doing here?" I snarl.

"Shay, she helped me get them out. If it wasn't for Sadie, I never would have made it off pack land with Brady and Colton."

Glaring at Sadie, I'm not sure I have it in me to forgive her.

Shay, if not for her, then what about Brady and Colt, who seem to need your help? Don't you think they would have come in with Maggie if they weren't hurt? Moon's pleading is the only thing that snaps me out of the fit of rage threatening to consume me.

"Where are they?"

"In the truck, Shay, I don't know if they are going to make it. Please, they need help."

Not needing further explanation, I raced to the truck only to come face to face with a living nightmare... Brady and Colton slumped in the backseat. I don't think I have ever seen someone so pale and still alive. The amount of blood covering their clothes and the back seat is startling. Discovering them like this, I realize the blood covering Maggie and Sadie came from them; this alone confirms they are running out of time.

"Get in," I yell as I call Ness's phone.

"I'm leaving in five minutes. Cool your hormones—"

"Ness," I yell as I throw the truck into reverse and peel out of my driveway.

"Shay, are you okay?" the urgency I feel leeches into her question.

"Ness, I'm on my way back to the pack. Get the hospital ready?"

"For what?" She may be asking questions, but I can hear her running to do what I asked.

"Brady and Colton are hurt. I'm on my way back in their truck with Maggie and Sadie."

"How bad."

"It may already be too late," I reply as the first tear tumbles down my cheek.

On our drive to the only place that may save and offer refuge to my previous pack members, Maggie continues to relay the details of what happened.

"Brady had him beat fair and square until Max stormed out into the ring and kicked Brady off Travis. When Colton tried to intercede on Brady's behalf, they attacked him. That fucker Max drove a blade into him so many times." I watch her in the mirror as she tenderly strokes Colton's face.

"Are you and Colt…." I don't know if I should ask her this now since I am unsure if he will pull through this.

"Together?"

"Yeah."

"We are, or we were. Please, Goddess, let it be we are," she cries as she lifts his still hand to her lips.

Realizing Maggie was incapable of finishing, Sadie cleared her throat and continued filling me in on what had happened.

"When Brady saw what Max did, he tried to rush him, but Travis stopped him when he drove a blade into his chest."

"How could Sebastian and Adela stand by while they tried to kill him?"

"I don't know, Shay. I wish I could tell you, but I can't."

"What happened next?"

Sadie looks sympathetically over her shoulder at Maggie, who is silently praying for a miracle. "They left Brady and Colton's bodies out on display as a warning to the other wolves who may object to the new regime. And they beat…." She stops and looks down at her hands.

"Me. They beat me and caged me while deciding what to do with me," Maggie says. This is the first time she has spoken that her words hold no emotions. Attacking the man she loves and her Alpha fills her with remorse and fear but threaten her, and she feels nothing. It's in this second I know Maggie is now more like me than I ever would have wanted.

"I couldn't stand by and do nothing, so I broke Maggie out, and then we drug Colt and Brady for almost a mile to a truck I hid."

"I'm sorry to pull you into this, but we didn't know where else to go," Maggie's voice is little more than a whisper now as she continues to stroke Colt's face and hold Brady's hand.

"We drove night and day to get here." This is the last thing either of them says for several minutes. Until Sadie clears her throat.

"Shay?"

"Yeah."

"I wanted to say.... Can you.... I mean, I know I owe you—"

"You don't owe me anything. Not anymore. Not after you risked your life to save them. We're square," I tell her as I take her trembling hand in mine.

"Thank you," she murmurs.

Three minutes later, I skid to a stop to find not just Ness waiting on us but Foster, Finch, and the rest of the pack.

*****

Brady

I have brief memories of falling. Of overwhelming pain. Of concern for my best friend, Colton. Of Maggie crying. But mostly, it's darkness and quiet because even Shade had gone silent. When I did come to, it was only because the pain was so excruciating it took everything in me to hold in my screams.

I also recall flashing lights and swaying that only comes from being in a moving vehicle. Then back to prolonged periods of nothing.

I believe my end has come when the sweetest sound I have ever heard invades my dreams. It's calming and comforting. It's almost as if I finally found the place I was always meant to be.

I cannot say how long I drift between life and death, but when I finally open my eyes, I know I survived Travis and Max's attack. I'm in a hospital, although not the one on my pack lands or the one we donate funds to. No, this place is unknown, and I'm not afraid to admit my heart jumps into my chest when I look over to find Foster sitting next to me.

"Hey man, welcome back."

"How-how did you get here?"

"I didn't come to you. You're on my pack land."

"How?"

"Maggie and Sadie," I vaguely remember being drug by Sadie. In my confused oxygen-starved state, I thought she was taking me to my grave, but I guess she saved me. I admit, after everything I have said about her, it's a tough pill to swallow, knowing she is the one who rescued us.

"Are they...." I can't seem to make myself ask if they made it.

"Recovering, but better off than you."

"They were injured as well?" I ask as I attempt to sit up, but the pain halts any thoughts of this.

"Maggie was attacked by the same assholes. Sadie hurt her leg while dragging you through the forest, but her wolf helped heal her once she could shift."

"Is Shay?"

"Sleeping over there on the couch. She hasn't left the room since we brought you in." Looking over in the direction he pointed, I find Shay curled up with a blanket covering her.

"She's got a soft heart."

"That she does," Foster confirms as he shifts his attention over to his sleeping mate. The thought of a mate brings the same warm feeling I had every time I heard the faint words of encouragement. It had to be Shay I heard all those times. My heart squeezes, thinking I will never have what she found with Foster, but how could I ask her to choose me when Foster took care of me when I needed it most?

"You're awake," I smile at Shay as she climbs off the couch, wiping the sleep from her eyes. She comes over and squeezes me in a tight hug before moving over to sit on Foster's lap.

They tell me everything that happened after Travis stabbed me. Thank Goddess, Maggie thought to bring us here; otherwise, there's no telling what would have happened.

"Is Mags with Colt?" Shay and Foster exchange a quick glance before Foster responds.

"No, she's out on the ridge."

"Ridge?"

"It's a scenic spot near here."

"Well, help me out of bed. I want to wake my brother up," I say with a laugh as I toss the blanket aside.

"Brady." Something about the way she placed her hand on my arm and said my name caused my heart to speed up.

"Shay, where's Colton?"

Shay takes my hand, and even before she tells me, I already know when I look up and find tears filling her eyes, "Our healers did everything they could, but his injuries.... I'm sorry, Brady. Colt didn't make it."

Note from the Author: As much as I hate killing off characters that people love, there comes a time when you need to do this for the storyline's progression. I'll miss writing Colt, but I needed to give Brady something other than Alpha to fight for. Hope you enjoyed season three and Foster and Shay's budding relationship. I also hope you enjoyed getting some other characters' perspectives; this will continue into the next season. Season four is currently the last planned season for Shadow's Moon, but I am planning a spinoff with Atlas and his story. Until we meet again, Happy Reading.

Also by *Marcelle Valentine*

Scarred by Fate Series

Ritual Nightmare
Breaking Purgatory
Fate's Ritual
Opposing Tartarus
Sacrificial Endings

The Ash Rock Series

Shadow's Moon Season One
Shadow's Moon Season Two
Shadow's Moon Season Three
Shadow's Moon Season Four

Arrival of the Four Horsemen Series

Death's Inquest
Pestilence's Judgment
War's Verdict
Coming Soon Famine's Punishment

Kindle Vella

Shadow's Moon Season One through Four
Seized by Sin
Silverwood Throne

Teaser

Betrayal brought me to this world. Henley keeps me here.

When my father falls ill, I soon discover this betrayal will cost me more than my father. I am forced to leave the fae realm I love behind to track the one responsible for this and protect my best friend. Navigating through this new realm, I am intrigued by Henley, the mortal woman I recruited to aid me in my search for Ayaan. She is everything I shouldn't want but can't resist.

As we work together to save my father and the fae realm from a looming threat, our attraction grows stronger. But the closer we become, the more I realize Henley has secrets of her own. Secrets that could destroy her and shatter everything I once thought I wanted.

Our attraction is like a flame burning brighter every day, but will it be enough to conquer the obstacles we face? Or will the weight of our past keep us from what we both desire?

Join Atlas and Henley on this steamy adventure as he battles to save the Silverwood Throne and his growing attraction for Henley. Return of the Fae Prince is a fantasy romance novel for adult readers.

Acknowledgments

When I began this project, I figured it would be a short story, something I could use as a starting point on Kindle Vella. I never knew how much I would learn to love the characters or how much they would have to say. Currently, season three is underway on Kindle Vella, and what I imagine is the fourth and final season releasing this Spring 2023. Each season will come to Kindle and Kindle Unlimited 30 days after the season completes on Vella. If you decide you cannot wait to continue their story, jump over to Kindle Vella to catch up with the gang from Ash Rock.

My deepest heartfelt thanks go out to every reader who took a chance on an unknown author and gave this series a chance. I hope you got lost in their world, if only for a minute in time.

I could not have completed this without the people who supported me, including my beta readers, my niece Ashley, my mom, and my daughter Melanie. Everything you each did to help me bring this project to life is something I could never say thank you enough. You each poured your time into this to help me make it something worth reading.

I have several projects currently underway, with the first one in my horsemen series, Death's Inquest, is available now.

Thank you to my husband and everyone else in my family who have been my biggest cheerleaders. I love every one of you.

And finally, to every author that has ever put pen to paper, fingers to keyboard, whose work only inspired me more to follow this dream, I hope I do not disappoint.

Thank you
Marcelle

Newsletter

Consider visiting my website and signing up for my newsletter to receive updates on this series and all my future projects.

www. marcellevalentine.com

Please consider leaving a review on Amazon and Goodreads if you enjoyed the book. Any thoughts are appreciated and will only help me improve the story. Reviews also provide new readers with a way to find my books.

You can also follow me on social media

Facebook
Goodreads
Instagram
TikTok

About the Author

Marcelle Valentine has long been an admirer of creating worlds in which people can get lost. From a young age, her active imagination took her on epic journeys to faraway places where troubles and friendships abound. After discovering the intriguing world of Paranormal/Fantasy Romance, which stirred up memories of all those distant places and friends, her desire to write returned. She invites you to travel with her during these journeys and get lost in a world with friends, enemies, and lovers, all firmly rooted in the supernatural realm. Marcelle is the author of the Scarred by Fate Series and the episodic series Shadow's Moon. She lives in Ohio with her husband. She has two children, three grandchildren, and one lovable, lazy Great Dane.

Marcellevalentine. com

Facebook

Twitter

Goodreads

Instagram

TikTok

www.ingramcontent.com/pod-product-compliance
Lightning Source LLC
Chambersburg PA
CBHW061239170626
46809CB00007B/2746
* 9 7 8 1 9 5 8 1 5 4 2 4 3 *